BLUESMAN

BLUESMAN

Fred Steen

JANUS PUBLISHING COMPANY
London, England

First published in Great Britain 1998
by Janus Publishing Company Limited,
Edinburgh House, 19 Nassau Street,
London W1N 7RE

www.januspublishing.co.uk

A CIP catalogue record for this book
is available from the British Library.

ISBN 1 85756 353 0

Phototypeset in 11 on 13 Garamond
by Keyboard Services, Luton, Beds

Cover design Nick Eagleton

Printed and bound in Great Britain by
Antony Rowe Ltd, Chippenham, Wiltshire

However, there is one exception to the above. I have mentioned the names of some of the great blues persons, and sometimes the titles of those songs and or materials most associated with their names and, in mentioning or referring to the song titles, portions of certain blues, or gospel songs, or works. That is my humble and sincere attempt at trying to honour those great blues and gospel singers. The mentioning of their names and music is in no way intended to downgrade or dishonour them or the music. With all my heart and soul, I only wish to tell the world about their music, and of their timeless and extraordinary contributions to the legacy and legend of the blues.

In truth, I have come to honour them.

Fred Steen, 2 November 1995

Dear Grandpa (Buddy)

I am writing this book in your loving honour, and I'm also trying in my humble way to honour all your old friends. Those great Bluesmen who you made it possible for me to walk along side them on the lonesome road of life for a short time. You placed me in the shadows of the true legendary Bluesmen of our times, so that I could hear them sing and play as only they could.

It is indeed an honour, and fills my heart with pride, to know that I was with you when you played the jooks, weddings, funerals and street corners of almost every little town in the delta. Also, we played and sang our way from Cairo, Illinois, down to New Orleans, and from Montgomery, Alabama, all the way over to Dallas, Texas.

Grandpa, I beg the dear Lord to grant you your guitar, your harp, and a pint of good sealed whisky.

I love you always
Sonny

13 June 1995

Contents

'One More Time'

Chapter 1

Shady Grove

It was a hot summer Sunday morning during the very height of the cotton picking season of the year. Throughout the Mississippi delta, the fields were all aglow with the white, plumy, open bolls of King Cotton.

Not too far from the little country town of Belzoni, Mississippi, was a large plantation, which boasted well over two hundred black farm workers, or slaves. Because of the first grade of cotton they produced, the plantation was well known, far and wide. But to those at the very heart of the matter, those who planted, chopped, and picked the cotton, the plantation was known simply as Lightcap's.

One of the nicest areas, or locations, found on Lightcap's was a beautiful grove of pretty green trees situated not too far from the Yazoo, and almost surrounded by a blanket of white cotton patches. And sitting almost in the centre of that grove of trees was a well-kept white church, complete with a small bell and tower.

The name of that church was, of course, Shady Grove Baptist Church. A stranger at shady grove would at first think that the church was a white folks' church. But it wasn't. No sir! Shady Grove was a Coloured folk church, a house of the good Lord. Why, that beautiful grove of trees and church was protected by a special grant from the big boss man and owner of the plantation.

Well, that Sunday was the first Sunday of the month, and the church was full to overflowing. Reverend Harris preached a sermon

1

that just lit everybody up, and shook the rafters. There was a feeling of a closeness with the Lord, and that feeling was all encompassing. Why, most of the good folk there that Sunday would surely say, 'God was smiling on Shady Grove that fine day.'

Oh, I tell you, that old church was just rocking with that old feeling of 'I done got over at last'.

Somewhere along the way, Sister Jessie Washington took the floor from the choir and she was putting her whole heart and soul into her very own version of that fine old gospel song, 'How 'bout you':

'I was standing at the bedside of a neighbour, and she was on her way. I say dear Lord take and use me, that is all that I can do, And I give my heart to Jesus. How about you? Oh how about you?'

It was quite impossible not to be moved. If you were there that day then you were moved, no doubt about it. Some of the good folk were shouting, some of the good folk were smiling, and some of the good folk were crying.

Delta tried, but he couldn't keep his seat. He just had to join his mama on the floor, and shout like most of the good folk of Shady Grove was shouting. His young voice blended in well with the beautiful country voice of his mother to sing:

'I say dear Lord take and use me that is all that I can do, and I give my heart to Jesus how bout you, oh how bout you . . .'

Even though it was during the time of broad daylight, a beautiful brown whip-poor-will flew into the church at Shady Grove that Sunday, and he gave his well-known cry, before he flew out again . . . Great God almighty, I done got over at last.

After the services were over, a lot of people came to hug Jessie and tell her how good she and her son could sing together. Now some folk thought Delta should surely be a country preacher, a man of the cloth. Goodness knows he had all the upbringing for it.

Of course, his dear mother felt the same way, and she wasn't at all happy that Delta, her oldest son, had chosen the 'other side of the road', and was nothing but a Blues singer.

She prayed to the good Lord that he would see his mistake and turn to the 'right side of the road,' and preach the Gospel according to Paul.

2

But no, he played that old guitar and harp every single minute he had the chance, just singing and playing the blues. She told him, the good Lord would catch up to him some day.

Jessie was real sorry that his run-a-round daddy was the first to teach him to play the guitar and sing the Blues. 'Lord knows that was the only thing his daddy ever gave him, before he went on down that lonesome road.'

And it didn't help matters none that the boy's grand-daddy was also an honest to goodness Bluesman in his own right. Plus they lived in the same house, it was impossible that what his grandpa had wouldn't rub off on Delta, and it did.

Buddy, that was his grandpa's Bluesman name, really taught Delta to play the guitar, the harp, and sing just like the old time greats. Delta could sing like Charley Patton, Blind Lemon Jefferson, Big Bill, or Leadbelly, and his harp was pure Sonny Boy, 'cause Buddy had often let Delta hear them play and sing. In the flesh, or in the spirit.

Folks around there gave RW the nickname of 'Delta Sonny' and the name stuck. Everyone had long since forgot his real legal name of Roosevelt Lincoln Washington, or for short, RW. On the other hand, her father carried his Blues name of 'Buddy Washington' for most of his life, and now RW was Delta Sonny.

Still, she couldn't help but feel a great pride in the fact that her son was turning into a 'Real Bluesman'. On the way back home she decided not to talk about his becoming a preacher. Instead, they talked about what to cook for dinner, and where his grandpa was getting his regular supply of White Lightning.

Jessie's mother and father went down to Silver City to visit a sick friend. So she and Delta was home by themselves. Jessie felt a great satisfaction in the sure knowledge that Delta would help her around the house and do the chores.

They were indeed lucky to have one of the nicest houses on Lightcap's, but that nice house brought along with it a lot of acres of cotton they had to produce. At first it wasn't too hard, when the family was all together.

But then her daughter, Thelma Jean, got the hots for a married man, and she ran off somewhere with him. After that, BC, her younger son, jumped a fast freight train headed for Chicago, and once he left that was four less hands to do the work, and placed an additional burden on those left to carry the load, which was really designed for at least six people, not four.

The work load was far too much for the four of them, so Buddy went personally to see old man Lightcap about taking a few acres off their backs. But before Mr Lightcap could answer, Mr Bob, the big boss man, said right off the bat, 'No!'

So they still had all that cotton to bring in. Buddy and Jessie were getting along in years, and no longer able to pull their full load. With those sad thoughts in her mind, Jessie just had to smile with the satisfaction that 'the Lord will make a way somehow...'

And I said to myself take courage,
Oh, the Lord will make a way somehow.

Chapter 2

Dues

The Washington family was indeed very lucky to get the house they had, because there were two other families who were qualified, and wanted it. But Buddy impressed old man Lightcap more than the other household leaders, so they got the place.

There was enough room so there was good places to sleep for Grandpa and Grandma, her and Thelma, and Delta and BC. The kitchen was separate from the house, and they had their own well from which the water was always cool and sweet.

Buddy and Delta patched the roof, fixed the floor near the fireplace, built a small barn, and a nice chicken house. The outhouse was situated a comfortable distance from the house and had a wood door instead of a burlap bag. The wood door kept snakes and other unwanted and uninvited guests out. It wasn't nice when you ran out there at night and you really had to go, and when you pulled the sack aside you found a mean old rattler was there ahead of you, and you had to fight him before you could do your business.

Of course the big house was on the positive side. Now the negative side was they were so deep in debt to the landowners that they could never get free. They would all surely die there on Lightcap's, picking cotton, crying and dying.

'Oh well!' Jessie said, as she let out a long sigh, and tried real hard to smile. 'Maybe BC was better off up there in Chicago. They said there was always work in the stock yards.' She managed a little better smile, when she also remembered that folks said that you could ride the bus or streetcar and sit wherever there was a vacant seat, and all the houses had toilets inside.

She tried to imagine what it would be like to live in a steam-heated apartment, and have the bathroom right there, to be warm in the winter months, without burning the front portion of your legs so much they looked like burned fat back.

One moonlit night shortly after supper, both Grandma Clara and Jessie suddenly felt as if they were being savagely beaten. When the almost Physical feelings, or Premonitions struck them, Clara was in the kitchen washing the supper dishes, and Jessie was outside feeding old Rattler, the family's hound dog. Both mother and daughter actually staggered and grunted in pain.

They acted as if they were actually under an assault, and being mentally and physically struck about the head and shoulders. Clara cried out and had to sit down before she fell down. Jessie leaned against the side of the house.

It was all so real. Somewhere, and at that same instant in time, BC or Thelma was being beaten to an inch of their life. Jessie's hands shook violently and she dropped the plate she brought the dog's food in. She struggled back to the porch and sat down, exhausted and in mental pain. Jessie looked at herself to see if she was bleeding.

After about five or ten minutes her mother came to join her on the porch. It wasn't necessary for them to tell each other of their extraordinary experience, or premonitions. They each knew full well what the other had gone through.

They looked at each other and without words they agreed not to tell Buddy and Delta what just happened to them.

After sitting quietly for a little while, and before the skeeters got extra bold, they went quietly to bed. The next day was on the way, morning would be there all too soon and with it they would be right back out in the blazing hot sun. Picking and crying.

Jessie found it hard to sleep, the tears in her eyes just wouldn't stop flowing. Somewhere around two o'clock in the morning she dropped off to a fitful semi-sleep. Her frail body was so tired, and her mind was almost numb from trying to determine which of her children was due to die.

Like mothers all over the world, Jessie knew exactly what her premonition meant. She just didn't know which of her wayward children she was going to bury.

The first faint sound, and old Rattler moving to the front door, brought her fully awake. She felt the weight of the world come to rest on her heart and shoulders.

'Oh, Dear God, No! Please God, no' she silently screamed.

For some unknown reason everyone in the house came awake, even though it was somewhere around three o'clock in the morning.

There it was again! A distinct sound. Like something being drug slowly across the front yard. That sound was accompanied by a distinct whimper, like the motion was causing someone great pain.

Then it was on the front porch. The slow dragging and whining. There came also the feeling of great fear, everyone was afraid to move.

Old Rattler, who normally slept in the kitchen, ran the rest of the way to the front door, and barked, but not in anger, because he was wagging his tail in a friendly motion. Then he threw his head back and let out the most pitiful whine they had ever heard. The dog's baying and howling caused their blood to run cold, and their flesh to break out in cold bumps.

Great God almighty, what a time.

What in the name of God was on their front porch? There it was again. Only that time it was much louder and more distinct. There was something distinctly human, and recognisable about the voice. Still they were frozen with the fear of what it was.

The dragging slowly proceeded across the porch toward the front door, accompanied by the terrible howling of the dog, and the thump, thumping of their hearts in unison.

'Mama. Mama. It's me, Mama,' the almost inaudible voice cried. Jessie felt a great pain in her chest. Her legs wouldn't move. Her mouth worked, but there was no sound, no sound coming from her lips at all.

Buddy jumped out of bed and grabbed his shot gun. Delta came with his old rabbit hunting stick ready to fight off whatever was at their door. Both he and Buddy thought it may be a cruel trick being played on them by the Klan. After all he and Delta was on the hit list of the local Ku-Klux-Klan. Delta had received a Warning from them because he was seeing too much of a certain white girl.

'Mama! Oh God, dear Mama, y'll come on and see about me,' the voice cried loud and clear . . .

'Y'll come on see bout me!' That time the words were most distinct, the voice was a little closer to the front door, and came in between the mournful howling of old Rattler.

'Daddy, y'll get out my way! That's BC's voice, that's my baby's voice, I would know it anywhere. Y'll move back!' Jessie pushed her way past her father and son, then she flung open wide the front door and screen. Once outside she let out a gut-wrenching scream that tore at the hearts of the rest of her family, even old Rattler felt the pain.

'Oh my sweet Jesus, BC! Oh God, oh my dear child, what have they done to you?' She fell down to her knees and held the huddled mass in her arms.

The remainder of the family rushed out to gasp in horror at the mass of humanity sprawled in pools of fresh blood. By that time someone had the presence of mind to light a lamp and there, on the well-worn porch and bleeding like a stuck pig, was Delta's younger brother, Benjamin (son of the right hand) Charles Washington, and believe me, any resemblance to his brother BC was purely coincidental. BC's hair was a cap of matted black blood and encrusted over his bloated face was some of that same blood.

BC's face was beaten to the point that even his own mother was having trouble recognising him. Both his eyes were almost totally swollen shut, and bloody saliva and froth dropped from his horribly mutated lower face. That his jaw was broken, or shattered, was quite evident to all.

His ruined lips were mashed all over his face. He let out a low long painful moan, and collapsed face first on the porch. Buddy and Delta gently carried him into the kitchen and laid him on the table.

BC stunk of urine, faeces, stale blood, sweat, tears, blood, and only God knew what else. Clara Bell Washington almost passed out from the sad sight of her grandson lying stretched out on the kitchen table. More dead than alive, most decidedly.

It was most plain that BC had dragged himself most of the way from the railroad tracks all the way home, and that was some ways to come on his hands and knees. The palms of his hands were a mess, and his knees all bloody...

Such a trip would require superhuman effort, considering the fact that he was busted up the way he was. BC came home on instincts, and the super power that sometime drives the animal to come home to die.

His mother knew that fact, still she had to try. Time was of the essence, and Jessie took command, trying to snatch his life from the cold hands of old Death. 'Buddy, I need some hot water fast! Mama, you help me get his clothes off. Delta, you go like the wind and fetch me Mama Zula. Tell her my child is dying.'

Delta hit the front porch only once, and ran like the wind off into the darkness of the delta night.

Later, when he and Mama Zula approached the house, she suddenly stopped dead in her tracks and pointed her finger at the top of the house and said, '*Shikwembu! Tsu Tsu Tsuuu! Abina! Hi Sona!*'

At that same time the old woman grabbed Delta's arm and then said in English, 'Ain't no more need to hurry boy. Your brother is already down to the river, and the ferry master is helping him aboard that mighty ship of our ancestors.'

Minutes before he slipped away, BC had a clear mind, and told his mama what brought him to that sad state. He told her that his killers were 'five or six railroad dicks who caught him up around Clarksdale, pulled him off the freight and beat him to death'.

He also told her about the Old North State tobacco sack that was tied around his waist and hung down between his legs like he had two sacks. The little cloth sack contained eight twenty-dollar bills, five ten-dollar and seven one-dollar bills.

They buried Benjamin Charles (BC) Washington in the shade of a big tree at the Shady Grove Cemetery. Less than two years later they also buried Clara Bell Washington not too far from her

9

grandson. She too, was a victim of the hard times, being black, living in the delta, and suffering the gross indignities of quasi slavery in the 1940s.

And in the land of Freedom.

Thelma came back home too. She was no longer young, pretty, and her once voluptuous body with those big hips that caused men to stare, were all gone. She was a mere ghost of her old self, down to skin and bone. Thelma had the pox, syphilis.

What happened to Thelma was an old story, acted out on the stage of life almost every day, and throughout the entire fabric of the lives of my poor people. The man she ran away with soon tired of her, and her womanly charms. Then he went on down the road followed, or pursued, by another fool.

After the loss of her first love, she took to sleeping with whoever wanted to sample her charms. Somewhere along the way she got burned, and burned real bad. She came down with syphilis, and the triple creeping crud. When she finally came to Brookhaven it was too late, they put a tube in her side and let her go home to her mama, home to die.

By that time she was ate up. Thelma died hard and screaming, 'Oh, if only I had listened to what my mama said. Please, dear Mother, forgive your child!'

They laid Thelma to rest next to BC, and not too far away from her grandmother in the quite serenity of Shady Grove.

Way before Jessie could get up off her knees, the Klan came one night to 'teach Delta a lesson'. Only he wasn't home, so in their anger and frustration they lynched his grandfather in his stead. 'Cause they didn't want to ride all the way out there for nothing...'

They lynched Nelson (Buddy) Washington right there before his daughter's eyes. Just before they rode off, Jessie got a real good look at their leader when the wind blew the conical hood and mask aside, which he was hiding behind.

That man was Mr Bob, the big boss man.

They laid Buddy Washington close to his family in Shady Grove, still another victim of the times of great sadness.

Jessie decided not to tell Delta that she knew the cowardly bastard who carried out the murder of her father and Delta's grandfather.

She didn't want to add to his already great burden that he shouldered. She just smiled and said aloud, 'What ever goes around, comes around.'

By that time old Delta was a Bluesman in his own right, and when he played her favourite tune which was called 'Haunting', oh she couldn't hold back the tears.

She went to see Mama Zula about getting even with Mr Bob.

One day some weeks after they buried Buddy, the big boss man came to tell Jessie that he was moving her and Delta into an old shot-gun shack on the other side of the plantation.

He laughed as if he was enjoying a private joke. On the other hand, Jessie already knew that it was the plantation owner, Mr Lightcap, who was trying to help her, not Mr Bob.

Shortly before leaving he told her to get him a cool drink of water from her well. She did, but Mr Bob didn't quite make it back to the big house.

They found him after the horse he was riding came home alone. Mr Bob was way out in one of the cotton patches, and slithering around on his belly like the snake that he was. He was frothing from his mouth like a mad dog, and baying at the moon.

He never got better, or spoke another word. Folks around those parts always said, 'It must have been something he drank.'

Jessie could then release *Nkunzi Ku Nyanyuka*, 'The fury of the bull.'

She would secretly smile when she heard folks make the remark about 'Something he drank.' Mama Zula knew her stuff. Silently she thanked that quiet little old woman who lived down in the hollow all alone. Or was she really 'all Alone'?

One day she gave Delta some of the money BC brought home. Jessie knew full well that it was time for him to hit the road. It was only a matter of time before the Klan would catch up to him, and there would be another fresh mound of earth at Shady Grove.

He gave his dear mother and best friend a warm hug, and Jessie held all she had left, her only son, real tight. Then she pushed him away from her and toward the main highway. 'Son, may the good Lord guide your footsteps, and some day I hope to hold you again in my arms. Till that time I shall hold you in my heart always and for ever. Go on now boy, take your guitar, your harp, and sing your Blues whenever, and wherever you can.'

Delta Sonny hit Highway 49 and went on down that lonesome road.

'I asked for water, and they gave me GASOLINE...'

Chapter 3

Black Beauty

Delta stood at the first major crossroads of his young life, and he stood there alone, except for the ghosts of the past, and his honourable ancestors. True, he knew that Jessie was always right there beside him, in spirit.

'It doesn't matter if your mother is alive or in the kingdom of God, always know one thing for certain, she is always right by your side.'

He stood there at the crossroads, his guitar slung across his back, neck down, and held in place by an old worn length of plow line. The black hat he wore was a hand-me-down and a gift from his Grandpa Buddy. The old blue serge suit he wore had seen better days, and was way overdue for an oil change. The shoes he wore were taken from the dead feet of his young brother. Jessie said it was better that he took them, 'Cause BC wouldn't need them in the kingdom of Great King Shaka, across the river.'

In his pockets were seven dollars and eleven cents. The small change consisting of two buffalo nickels and one Indian head penny. His money belt held the rest of his going-away money, which was forty-four dollars in small bills.

Plus, he wore around his neck a small Mojo or JuJu Bag made especially for him by Mama Zula. He was instructed 'Never to take it off till he was back home, and the Black Cat Bone was to be used only in hard times.'

13

His original plan was to go north to Chicago, and play on Maxwell Street. But then standing there at the crossroads something told him to go south instead. Besides he had a bad taste in his mouth about what happened to BC, and he really didn't want to go too far away from his mother. They were the only two left living from their family.

There was also another factor that caused him to change his mind. You know during those times a lot of the good coloured folks from the south of the country who went north to the Promised Land, tried hard as hell to leave the Big Foot Country behind. Way behind.

Often, that meant leaving their great heritage of the country Blues behind also. So maybe the good folks wouldn't want to hear 'Must I holler or must I shake 'em on down'.

Some of the good folks definitely didn't want to be from Mississippi. Anywhere, but not from 'Sippy'. Once they got off that 'Hound' they walked that walk and talked that talk. Real proper like. Call them country and you had to fight them. Razor or no razor.

'Don't you hear me talking to you pretty mama, Oh I ain't going down that big road all by myself. I ask for water and they gave me Gasoline!'

It's too bad some of the good folks didn't realise that you can get out of the country, but you can't get the country out of yourself.

So Delta headed south towards Jackson, and he also decided to stay away from the main roads and highways. He travelled the back gravel and dirt roads. 'Cause he knew that's where the real heart of the people who made up the delta were to be found. They were the real salt of the earth.

The first night out he slept in a cotton house, which was sitting way out in the fields by its lonesome. Except for three trees in the cleared area close by. One of the trees still had a pair of scales used for weighing the cotton hanging from a convenient limb.

Delta was pretty tired and down in heart when he climbed over the half door, but he cheered up a little when he found enough cotton to sleep on, and cotton sacks to keep the skeeters off him.

During that night his Grandma Clara came and told him 'not to go to Jackson just yet'.

Shortly before the light of the next day he quickly slipped away from the cotton house and was on his way again. A little later that same morning, he stopped in a cotton patch with some folks who brought their breakfast to the field with them. Of course they offered to share their meagre fare with him.

The flour bread hot cakes were excellent. Cooked in an old iron skillet with lots of grease and just the right amount of sugar was added to the dough so if you wanted to eat just the bread alone you could. Of course the molasses was homemade and good. The salt pork was fried hard and a strip of lean and strip of fat. That most excellent delta breakfast was all topped off with a tin cup of cold butter milk.

Oh I tell you, if it's possible to get a better breakfast I sure would like to know what it would be. Why some of the folks even gave Delta their meat skins to 'Tide him over', so when he said thanks and goodbye he had at least five good long meat skins to chew on.

He was fixing to play and sing for them, but they saw the old boss man coming and he decided to pass. They understood. One lady wanted to hear the 'Vicksburg Blues' and he promised her that he would come back and play for her another time.

Delta moved on to the main road and was almost out of sight within minutes.

Later that evening, somewhere 'long about seven-thirty, from the road he could see an old house. The place was badly in need of repair, and suggested there was no man to fill the bill. Smoke was coming out the kitchen chimney, which was a good sign, and a small boy wearing only a pair of bib overalls was in the back yard chopping wood.

A good look around the area showed the next closest house to be almost out of sight, and a small cotton house situated almost directly in between the two houses. Of course the rest of the area and as far as the eye could see, was cotton fields. To be sure, there was always the surrounding tree line that made you feel like you were in a great big bowl.

Delta was very tired after walking all day, not to mention he was

15

also very hungry. He ate the meat skins for dinner, and drank some water from a creek, but that didn't last too long.

He decided to try the house with the little boy chopping wood, and the smoke coming out the kitchen chimney, besides the other house was too far away, and BC's shoes were killing him.

His original plan was to go to the settlement in the hope of picking some cotton. That way he could earn a dollar a day, or a dollar a hundred. But the smoke from the kitchen chimney was closest to a bird in hand...

The dog started barking first, and the boy chopping wood stopped working to watch him as he approached. Clearly, the boy was happy like he was expecting someone. But when he could plainly see Delta, the young lad couldn't hide his disappointment. Still he greeted Delta with a big smile.

'Howdy do young fellow, folks call me Delta. What do they call you?' Delta said.

'Frank, my name is Frank Young. Are you a friend of my Daddy?'

'Well, no Frank, I'm sorry, I don't know your dad. I'm just passing by and I thought I would stop by here and ask directions to the settlement.'

Just about that time a woman stepped from the outhouse, which was located not too far from where Delta and the little boy were standing. The first full view of her said that she was some years older than Delta. Without saying anything, she went first to the wash stand and washed her hands, then she came directly to where her son and Delta were waiting.

'Mister, my Mama can tell you how to get to the settlement, but you can't make it before dark, even if you go through the cotton patches,' the boy said.

'Howdy stranger, can I help you?' the woman said. Yes, she was older than he, but her age only added to her natural beauty. Her ebony skin glistened with the sweat from her ample and womanly body, which was highlighted by the late evening sunlight from the fading day.

Her expression was very frank and she did not smile. Her big brown eyes reflected supreme confidence, no doubt about it she was a very strong woman. In the proud tradition of her African

16

ancestors. She was black and beautiful, she was beautiful and black. Truly a Black Beauty. Delta tried in vain not to look at her full woman's body squeezed into the old print cotton dress she was wearing. From the top of her head to the bottom of her bare feet, she was all woman. He noted that her strong legs were, as usual, marred with the burn scars caused from sitting too close to the fireplace on cold wint'ry nights.

With some visible effort, he managed to look her in the eyes. 'Well, Ma'am, I just stopped by to ask directions, I'm going on down to Jackson. I just thought I would make a little money picking cotton along the way.' He smiled

'What did you say your name is?' the woman asked.

'Delta, just call me Delta,' he said.

'Frank, you go check my fire, and put the skillet on with some water in it.'

'Yes'm,' the boy said as he ran to the kitchen.

'And Mr Delta, I wouldn't advise you to go down there tonight. We had some trouble there not too long ago, so your not being from around here could cause you to get hurt.'

'Well, ma'am ...'

'Josie, I'm Josie Young.'

'Well, Josie, I don't know anybody around here, like I said I'm just passing through.'

'Well, Mr Delta, it's about night, and I'm about to fix supper for me an' Frank. You're perfectly welcome to join us, if you want to.'

'Josie, I do thank you, and if I can put Fanny Mae, that's what I call my guitar, over there on the porch, I'll finish chopping this wood and help with the chores. Frank can tell me what needs to be done.'

'That's right nice of you, Delta. Frank will be right with you, meanwhile I'll rattle the pots and pans.' She took Fanny Mae and his coat into the house.

By the time they finished the chores Frank and Delta were fast friends. Delta listened to the boy talking about his dad, and came to the correct conclusion that the boy thought the world of his daddy. So while slopping the hogs, Delta thought it was OK to ask about the father.

17

The story was about the same story across the entire land; America was at war and most of the eligible men were answering the nation's call to arms, Frank's Daddy included. There was an older brother who had already put the cotton sack down in exchange for a wrench. Josie's older son was in Detroit, and soon as he had the money and a place, she and Frank planned to join him.

The Great Migration north to the Promised Land was about to begin. The prime movers of the grand old south were already slipping away to the freedom and factories of the north.

Before their fine supper of freshly cut fried corn, golden-brown salt pork, and butter milk fist biscuits was over, Josie had to light the lamp so they could see. During the meal she asked Delta a lot of questions, and some of the questions were most direct.

He answered her questions as frankly as he could, only hesitating a little when she asked his age. It bothered him that he didn't want her to know his correct age, and he was not sure why he added a few years when he gave her a false number. He felt ashamed right away, 'cause he knew deep down inside that somehow, she knew he lied about his age.

Also during the conversation at supper he figured out that she and Frank were planning to steal away north in a few days. All the indicators were there, plus the fact that while they were feeding the dog, the boy let it slip that a cousin was going to keep the dog.

After supper he pitched in and helped to clean the kitchen. It was plain that she appreciated his help. Once the kitchen was all clean, she told Delta that he could sleep in the bed with Frank, or they could make a pallet on the floor for the boy. He told her if it was OK, he would just as soon share the bed with Frank, it wasn't necessary to put the boy on the floor.

The heat of the day still lingered inside the tin-roofed house, creating sort of an oven. So they went outside to sit in the cool of the night on the front porch. The skeeters wasn't too bad, so they just sat quietly for a few minutes, each with his and her own thoughts. Josie knew Delta was younger than what he told her. On the outside she accepted it, on the inside she knew he wasn't much older than her boy up there in Detroit.

To change her thoughts, she asked Delta to play something for her. Frank volunteered to get Fanny Mae. It was a good feeling to hold his old guitar, and he took some few minutes to refashion the piece of wire he used to hold his harp around his neck so he could have his hands free to play. The floorboards of the porch was just right for him to stamp his foot to keep time and bass.

Frank sat close to Delta so he could watch him play. The night was pleasant, and there was a full moon. The scene was like something out of a Hollywood movie, and the delta night creatures provided backup for him with their nocturnal music.

'I'm a poor boy, long, long ways from home,' he began to sing and play.

From where he sat he could see the light shining through the window of the distant house down the line, and his thoughts went back home to his mother. He wondered if she was OK out there all by herself.

'Trouble in mind I'm blue, but I won't be blue always. Cause the sun gon shine in my back door someday...' His voice took on that long lonesome haunting quality, and the sadness of all those hard years in the cotton fields, plus the cruel and untimely death of those he loved so much just came rushing at him.

He sang the story of John Henry, and you could almost hear John Henry's hammer ringing.

Josie couldn't help herself, she couldn't hold still. Like black folk all over the world, when she heard and felt the rhythm of Mother Africa, her body began to move in time. It's quite impossible to sit still.

Have you ever noticed those people of African descent, and observed them when they hear the rhythm and the call of the drums of Home? From six to a hundred and six, they all have one thing in common, they start to move.

Well, anyway, Delta sang and played what he felt. Josie knew the feeling, and she knew he had come a long, long way. Her beautiful woman's body moved in time, even though she was sitting down. Her feet moved to the beat, and Delta knew she was enjoying his music.

He was doing 'Don't start me talking' when he noticed that Frank was asleep. His mother told Delta that little Frank picked a

19

hundred pounds of cotton that day; the young lad was passed out. She woke him up, and he told Delta how much he loved his music and went on off to bed. Josie checked on him and he was sleeping soundly.

She and Delta sat out on the porch for a few more minutes talking about the changing times. Then she excused herself to go wash up before bed; after she was finished he did the same thing. Frank was sleeping peacefully and sprawled on the bed under the mosquito net, anything short of an earthquake wouldn't wake him.

Delta laid down beside the sleeping boy. He was just dozing off, when a vision of womanly beauty stole into his view, then into his mind and heart.

Quietly, she raised the mosquito net and took his hand as she urged him to get out of the bed. She placed her finger to her lips in the signal for him to be quite so as not to wake her young son.

She led him to her bed, where he sat on one side and watched her standing in the shaft of cool golden moonlight flowing through the window and gently caressing her fine ebony body, as she let her old tattered housecoat fall to the floor.

Truly. He had never in his young life witnessed such a sight. His mind reeled, his mouth went dry, and his body reacted with the call of what was to be.

Her smooth black body was full, and rounded, her breast seemed to swell to almost bursting. Sweet Jesus, Josie was the epitome of the perfect woman. She turned slowly, allowing the moonlight to dance, and reflect off her beautiful glistening ebony body. So he could completely see her unashamed nakedness.

It was a ritual as old as man himself. One of those things that we do without ever being told how to do them. The call of the male feathered bird. The dance of fertility. The call of life continuing.

Delta had never seen so much at one time. His ears popped, and his sight was blurred, speech was impossible. Somewhere in time, and after she was satisfied that he fully understood what she was offering him, and what his responsibility would be, she stood very still and looked directly into his wide eyes. Oh yes, and into his very soul.

He went to her, and was further mesmerised with the true

meaning of her being. The sweet musk of her, and the salt of her tears, sent him flashing back to the beginning.

Delta took Josie in his arms and carried her over to the bed where there began the ageless call of life itself.

Whether it is more noble to confine oneself to the laws of the modern society. Or to revert to the beginning. To be a boy in the body and mind of a man, or a man in the body of a boy. That could be the question.

Are there any answers...

*   *   *

The morning calm brought with it a soft gentle breeze which carried the odours of the full bloom cotton, some of the smells from the garden, and some of those from the woods not too far away.

There was also the promise of another hot Mississippi delta day.

Josie fixed breakfast, and while she did even her son noticed the change in her, and the smile on her usually unsmiling face. Delta helped Frank with the morning chores, and they talked together about the future.

At breakfast they laughed and told jokes, after breakfast she fixed Delta some bread and meat to carry with him on his way. Too soon it was time for him to move on, it was time for them to part. Yes. He knew full well that once he was gone, he might never see them again. That's what made the pain so bad. The real world rushed in to embrace him.

Delta gave Frank ten dollars and made the boy promise not to tell his mother till he was long gone. Then he hugged Frank and the dog. He only touched Josie's hand and looked into her eyes; still, he thought he saw a tear.

True, her hands were calloused and the skin broken in places from the sharp spikes of the cotton bolls, yet there was a gentleness of her touch unknown to him until the night before.

Delta Sonny came there a boy and was transformed by a woman into a man. She was indeed and truly a Black Beauty if ever there was one...

Chapter 4

Rolling Fork

'You got me way down here in Rolling Fork just to make me walk the log. Baby, please don't go, cause I love you so, baby please don't go.'

There was a little house right outside Rolling Fork where an old Legend Bluesman lived in semi-retirement. That old Bluesman was a dear and true friend of Delta's grandfather; he and Buddy took their Blues as far north as Canada, and south to Mexico. They were some of the original and true practitioners of the art.

Buddy had told Delta to go down to Rolling Fork shortly before the cowards in the white sheets murdered him. His grandfather even gave him some secret recognition words to say to the old Bluesman. That way Buddy's old friend would know that Delta was who he said he was.

The recognition words was simply to say, 'Peetie Wheatstraw the Devil's Son-in-Law.' Now, you see, that little diddy made it possible for Delta to show what he could do, and to strut his stuff before a Bluesman who was already a Legend in his own time.

It was kind of hard for Delta to really play well before an audience of one. But he knew that one was like the ears of all the people. Boy, old Delta was as nervous as a whore in church. He couldn't get his little piece of board right on the floor, and the homemade wire harness around his neck to hold his harp just wouldn't stay in place.

'Now come on, Junior, grab a hold of your dick, and get yourself in order. I ain't going to bite you, yet. But if you plan to get up in front of people who gave you their hard-earned money, Boy, you damn well got to do something, and do it right.

'Now, damn you, Boy, play!' the old man yelled at him. 'Don't waste my time, I'm going to listen to you no matter what. Cause I surely do owe your Grandpappy Buddy. I remember the times he saved my butt more than once. I promised him long time ago that if he ever sent you to me I would see that you got off on the right foot.'

'Well, I'm a po boy long, long way from home,' Delta began to play and sing. It didn't take him long to get the feeling, and the stage fright flew right out the window. It was like his Grandpa was right there with him, and Delta finished 'Po Boy' and went right on into a song he had only heard his Grandpa sing.

'Oh, jack of diamonds, you jack of diamonds.' That song really brought an unexpected reaction from the old Bluesman. When Delta began to sing 'Jack of Diamonds' the old man quickly turned his face away, but not before Delta saw the pained expression the old Legend was trying to hide.

Plainly, the song brought back some painful memories to the old man. Delta continued to play and sing. Of course, over the years he changed some parts of the original version as taught him by Buddy, and added a nice long harp solo.

'Honey, bring me my guitar!' the old man yelled to the woman in the next room, and she almost ran to him bringing his well-worn musical instrument to him. And with a smoothness brought on through years of practice, the old Legend took his guitar and joined Delta in the last portion of 'Jack of Diamonds'.

After that, Delta wasn't playing for the approval or disapproval of the old man that Buddy wanted him to play for. No! He was playing for the pleasure of playing, and the old man joined him in that pleasure. They played because it was right. They played because that was what old Bluesmen did whenever and wherever they met.

That fact was traditional.

'Must I holler or must I shake 'em on down.' They sang and played like they been together for a long time. As it always happened, before long there was an entire band sitting in the room.

23

Someone set up a homemade drum set, which consisted of old apple crates, pots, pans, and a small wash tub. The bass was a wash tub turned upside down on the floor with a single string threaded through the bottom centre, and held taut by a stout willow pole attached to the side of the tub. There was a washboard player, a jug blower and a blind man who could really play his harp.

'If you see my milk cow, please drive her home, cause I ain't had no good milk and butter since she been gone.'

Sometimes Delta led and sometimes the Legend led. Oh, they just got on down. People came out of nowhere, and soon the joint was as tight as a dick's hat band. Someone held a fruit jar to his dry lips, and he sucked down a good amount of some pure White Lightning that curled his toe nails, and blurred his vision. And the crystal-clear liquid was so smooth, he couldn't feel it going down, but once it hit bottom he knew it was there, for sure.

They did 'Devil in the Woodshed', 'Baby Please Don't Go', 'Make Me Down a Pallet', 'Little Queen of Spades', 'Wild Cow Moan', and many more of the old time country Blues that were the mainstay of those times.

When Delta took a breather he was happy to smell catfish frying and corn bread baking, with those wonderful aromas tickling his nose, and the fact that the place was packed told him that a Saturday night fish fry was in full swing.

Someone started, 'Good Evening Little Schoolgirl', and somewhere along the way he realised that Sonny Boy was standing right beside him.

That was the time that he realised everything was going to be all right.

It was way past midnight, and he was bone weary, but happy. His fingers were greasy from eating hard-fried delta-style catfish and corn bread. The peppers were outstanding, and he knew he would be feeling them again.

He was sitting on the back porch talking with a pretty local girl when the old man came to sit beside him. The girl disappeared immediately without a word.

'Listen, Junior, you got your granddaddy's style, and you got a whole lot of your own. But don't you forget you got a long way to go before you reach the Upper Room. But there is no doubt in my mind that you will reach it. So I'm giving you my blessings, I want you to know the fellows we just played with tonight all said that you are OK.

'There is a jook tomorrow night over near Holly Bluff, and one will be going on out from Pocahontas. Some of us are going to play Holly Bluff, and maybe on down to Pocahontas. From there we will spend the night in Jackson.

'Would you like to go?'

By that time Sonny Boy and a guy with a peg leg joined them, and Delta Sonny knew he was on his way...

Delta rode in the car with his new mentor and the peg leg guy. The car belonged to Sonny Boy, and was a late model Ford complete with a radio. Right outside Rolling Fork and from an old lady who lived in a shot-gun house not too far from the road, they bought three mason jars of good peach-coloured White Lightning. Each pint-size jar was almost full of that golden goodness, and they started right away to take one of the jars down to size.

Well, you see, old Delta knew he couldn't hold up to the company he was keeping. That peach-coloured corn squeezing packed a mean punch. Sure it was like sneaky Pete smooth and mellow, and all right, long as you were sitting down. But don't stand up...

Old Delta knew full well how much he had riding on his upcoming performance. He didn't need no scrambled brain, and he wasn't up to no heavy drinking. So when one of the jars was passed to him he only pretended to take a slug, and passed the jar on to the next man.

The old man looked at Delta and smiled his approval, he knew Delta wasn't drinking.

On the other hand, the Guy with the peg leg was making up for what Delta didn't drink. Watching that guy suck on the jar, Delta made a mental note to check if the peg leg was really hollow.

The jook was on a plantation that was really closer to Valley Park than Holly Bluff. But still they got there well before the guests arrived. The big boss man gave the organisers permission to use a covered hardstand which was a part of the gin, and normally used to store bales of cotton awaiting shipment. There was a makeshift bandstand which was arranged atop some bales of cotton, and there were electric lights, also compliments of the gin and the big boss man.

After a little haggling over how much money they would receive, they got on down to doing what they did best. There were two or three wash tubs full of iced-down Jax Beer and of course off a little ways in to the woods were two wooden buckets hanging from a tree.

Now those wooden buckets were full of good old delta White Lightning, and hanging close to each bucket was a tin, or gourd dipper, to be used to convey the elixir of eternal youth to your mouth.

Oh, the joint was jumping. And the good folks were getting on down!

Even the mosquitoes were getting drunk. Of course some of the good folk brought their own. One guy had a hot water bottle full of Stump Juice, and the bottle had a rope tied through the hole in the rubber bottom, and slung across his shoulders. The end with the cap and rubber hose with the shut-off valve he carried in his mouth like smoking a pipe.

All he had to do was release the valve, and suck. It was a good idea, but he got loaded and passed out. Somebody took his rubber bottle and did in what was left, so all was happy.

The band of True Bluesmen played one song after the other, and the good folk danced their appreciation. The big boss man eased on to the jook and got on down like the coloured folks were doing. He was lit up like a Christmas tree, and greasy from the bar-b-cue like everyone else.

One of the players on the bandstand got drunk and fell off on his head. It was plain he wasn't going to play any more that night.

'Junior Washington, get your young butt on up here and take his place,' Sonny Boy yelled to Delta, after which Delta climbed up on the bandstand and moved smoothly into the heart of the matter. The old man let Delta lead, and he broke out into 'John Henry, that steel driving man'. The crowd loved it, he added a little holler and followed with his harp.

First, he was hesitant to play his harp, what with Sonny Boy the old master standing right next to him, but then he decided to let it all hang out. Sonny Boy followed him, and they played real good together.

Somewhere around two a.m., they were loading the car in preparation for moving on. Delta's cut of that night's taking was two dollars and thirty-five cents. Which wasn't too bad considering that he ate all he could hold, and drank his fill, plus he got to play beside some of the true legends of the Blues circuit.

And he met an old gal who wanted to take him home. That was nice but there was one slight problem. You see, her old man was bigger than King Kong, and twice as mean.

Why, that old boy looked like he could bite the heads off railroad spikes, and someone had to hold him when he shaved. Just to keep him from killing himself out of pure meanness.

When Grave Yard Jones (that's what folks called him, on account he had sent a lot of men to the grave yard) saw his woman making eyes at Delta, he moved in very quickly.

A hush fell over that portion of the crowd who witnessed the little drama unfolding; they knew another poor boy was close to dying, if old Grave Yard got really pissed. That's when Sonny Boy stepped in and got Delta off the hook.

Now old Sonny Boy did some tall talking, and he also pointed out to Grave Yard that the old man was pointing a 38 Smith and Wesson directly at Grave Yard's big gut. Of course, it helped a lot when Grave Yard looked over and saw that Sonny Boy was telling the truth.

He saw that single deadly eye of the 38 looking right at him, even though the old man was holding the pistol so no one else could see it. Grave Yard saw it, and that was enough. He backed off.

The next day, Sonny Boy got Delta off to the side and talked to him like he was the Father that Delta never had.

'Now, Junior, you listen to me and you listen real good. You got to get out there on your own, and you ain't always going to have me and Pops to back you up. It's lucky we got the drop on that big bastard last night, otherwise he was going to eat you up. Boy, you got to get you an old pistol and keep it on you all the time. That's what we all do, 'cause you can never tell when you might need it.

'Also you got to work the streets, the jooks, the houses, funerals and whatever. There is no standard way to do it, whatever works for you is the right way. If you do something wrong, folks will let you know right away, make no mistake about that fact. You got to learn from your mistakes, 'cause sometimes if you make the same mistake twice that mistake may very well be your last mistake. You hear me, boy!

'Now, it's best to always keep moving, don't stay in one place too long, it ain't good for your health. Stay away from those old girls who make goo goo eyes at you. Always know the mere fact that they are there tells you that they are not alone, some old boy is watching his meat, and will shoot you, cut you, or beat your brains out to keep what is his.

'Now, if you do go home with some local gal, don't go to sleep, watch what you drink, and don't turn your back on no one. Do what you go there to do, and when you are finished, catch the first thing smoking.

'Now, Delta, I know you've met some of the best Bluesmen in the Mississippi delta, you've heard them sing an' play, and you've picked up from them, plus all that your Grandpa Buddy gave you. Sure there is a whole lot more for you to learn before you are gonna be a true Bluesman.

'Young fellow, we both know there is so much that I could teach you. But I'm going to stop here, and let the best teacher of all take over. Of course we both know the name of that Teacher is Experience.

'Now, Delta Sonny, you can be an even better Bluesman than your Grandpa Buddy ever was, all you got to do is put your whole heart and soul into what you do, and do the best that you can all the time. Oh, and one last word of advice, boy, don't you ever forget to take your young butt back home to see your mama.'

By the time Sonny Boy was finished talking to Delta they were joined by the old man, and he also had a few words of Survival Advice to pass on to Delta, that along with his blessing.

Delta Sonny had reached the 'The Man on Top of the Mountain in Rolling Fork', and he had successfully walked the log.

After that it was up to him. He decided to 'Reach up and grab iron...'

Chapter 5

Black Cat's Bone

Delta hitched a ride to Jackson where he found a bed at Mama T's Boarding House. The first afternoon of his first day in Jackson he worked the north end of Ferris Street, starting near the Big Four Barber Shop, then up to the Big Apple and settling down a few doors north of Pig Iron Ross's place.

He stood playing and singing under the streetlight till the bugs and gnats drove him away. Actually he was very pleased with the results of his first few hours out. The pocket which he kept his earnings in was growing heavy, sure he knew that it was only coins, nickels, dimes, pennies, and in some very rare instances someone may have given him two bits (a quarter, 25 cents). Still it was a start.

Just before the bugs drove him away, the lady from the house nearest the streetlight brought him a cold Jax beer and asked him to play 'Good Evening Little Schoolgirl'. He did and she stayed there till he was finished, before returning to her front porch. She suggested that he try the Jackson Country Club, which was located down the hill and in the woods not too far from the Pearl River.

The nice lady even arranged for her neighbour to drive him down to the home of the caretaker of the country club, who was a relative of hers.

Delta thanked her, and was off to play for some of the white elite of Jackson. Hopefully.

Once there he met Mr Dennis James and his wife, who were the club's caretakers, and Delta was happy to discover that Dennis was also an old Bluesman. He and Delta hit it off from the very start, and Dennis got permission for Delta to play and sing for the good white folks who wanted to hear him.

Delta played for them until around one o'clock, then he and Dennis played together till around three o'clock. By that time it was too late to go back to Mama T's, so Dennis offered him to stay the rest of the night with them, in their house up on stilts.

A few nights later, and remembering the good advice given to him by Sonny Boy and the old man, plus the fact that the police had already questioned him one time too many and asked him about his Draft Card, he knew it was time for him to move on down the line.

Delta's first thought was to go north to Chicago, but for some unknown reason he made the decision to go south to New Orleans. Some of the men who were living at Mama T's knew exactly what time, and what freight to catch out of the IC Yards of North Jackson, bound for New Orleans. They were more than happy to pass on some of their expertise to Delta.

He stood crouched in some tall weeds a few yards from the railroad tracks where the tracks curved and headed in a direction from which the engine would be heading off to his right, and the centre portion of the train would prevent the engineer, or the personnel riding the caboose, from seeing him as he grabbed iron.

His position was calculated so he could grab iron when the freight slowed for the curve after leaving Doodlesville, and before the engineer began to high-ball. It was just before complete darkness fell, the quietness of the late evening, and the sound of the engine approaching, heralded by the long doleful sound of the train's whistle. All the sounds of the moment, and the fact that he was fixing to grab iron, was most exciting.

There is something above and beyond about catching a fast freight in a curve, and listening to the clacking of steel against steel while the chugging of an old steam engine and the mournful sound of the whistle urges you on, to grab hold and become one with the great iron horse of the times. Once you first did it, you were hooked for life, the rush was worth every bit of the downside.

Sure, old Delta had enough money to catch him a Dog on down

31

to New Orleans. But to ride the rails, to grab the iron of a fast freight was also to feel the thrill of being in motion. It was the only way to go.

He climbed aboard, waited a bit, then he moved forward, just in case he was seen. He found an empty box car with only some mounds of trash inside, and the wall on one side of the car had a large hole clean through, a hole large enough for him to escape, if he had to.

Moving quickly, and with some efficiency, he arranged some of the trash so its location would benefit the position he planned to occupy near the hole torn in the box car wall. He was very careful to find a good position for his guitar, and to ensure the instrument would fit through the hole. Then he settled down to ride the rails on down to Cajun country. He was very tired and even though he tried not to, he was quickly fast asleep.

Fact was, that growing up black in the Mississippi delta was really what gave old Delta the warning signal, even in his sleep, that something was wrong. His Survival Instinct woke him up. His first stolen glance was to his guitar, and over to his escape hole.

You see, that hole in the wall was one of the main reasons he chose that particular car. And even though he hoped he wouldn't need it, it seemed like his planning was about to pay off.

He could feel and hear the train picking up speed, which told him the engineer had slowed down for a crossing or a curve. If the train slowed for a curve then it was very possible that someone jumped aboard. His early warning told him he was fixing to have company.

Even before the first of the two Bos swung lightly down into the slightly open doorway of the box car, he landed upright, and on his feet looking around. The other Bo came right after the first one.

The two men were so dirty, and the light so poor, that Delta couldn't tell right away if they were back or white, Friend or Foe.

The two men stood almost back to back and slightly swaying with the movement of the train. The fact that they were experienced Bos was so plain even a blind man could see it. Once they finished their visual inspection of the car, the one facing where Delta lay said something to his partner. They had a hurried conversation, then they started moving slowly towards where Delta lay, pretending to be fast asleep and unaware of their presence.

Fact was, he had his eyes almost closed and leaving only narrow slits so he could observe his new and unwanted guests. He was watching them since they jumped in the car. He chose that method to see what they were up to.

Folks will do a lot of strange things, specially when they think no one is watching. They often forget, someone will always see you...

The closer the two men came to where Delta lay, the more he was sure they didn't mean him any good. Also they were near enough for him to see they were white, and therefore bad news for him.

Of course that was not to say that all the white hobos were bad news, but the fact that he was who he was, and in the deep South, surely did stack the odds in their favour.

The two men came to stand over him, so close he could smell their stench. Why, those old boys hadn't had a bath since they were born; a good bath with some soap would kill them dead as hell. They looked at each other and smirked about what they had planned for their helpless victim.

Meanwhile, old Delta was just lying there. He was planning what to do to save himself, and trying hard to push away the visions still in his mind of what they did to his brother.

He remembered Buddy saying there were many problems that went along with riding the rails, or hitching a free ride on a freight train. That sometimes those problems could cost more than just buying a ticket.

First off, it was illegal.

If the railroad-personnel or crew aboard the train, or the railroad dicks (detectives) caught you, it was hell to tell the captain. You could wind up with a good beating, in jail, on the count farm, or even worse, you could wind up stone-cold dead.

All that was bad enough. But if you happened to be coloured, black, or/and a nigger. You not only had to watch out for the train crew, the railroad dicks and people in general. You also had to watch out for all the other hobos. Especially if they were white.

Old Jim Crow reached all the way down to the tramp level.

Sure, every now and then you would meet a Bo who was white

and didn't try to assert his white superiority on you. But, you know, those Now and Thens were few and far between.

'Wake up, Boy! You got yourself some company,' the larger of the two Bos yelled at Delta.

He came slowly awake, looking around as if he was confused, and when he gained eye contact with his new visitors, he showed the proper and expected fear in their presence. There was also the expected stupid smile disgracing his face.

He was doing exactly what they expected him to do, and in the process of doing that, he was in fact gaining the upper hand. For you see, they automatically lowered their guard, accepting him and his Act, as just another scared nigger.

Sometimes the best defence is to make your enemy think you are defenceless.

'Bubber, you can tell this boy is kind of new at riding the rails, and not too bright. Any fool knows better than to go to sleep in a box car all by himself. That's why we always travel in pairs,' the big hobo said to his sidekick, as he grinned down at the cowering young black man in the dirty black hat.

Still old Delta pretended to 'know his place' and accept the fact that he was in the presence of his betters.

'What's your name, boy?' The smaller of the two men spoke for the first time. His voice was soft and kind of squeaky, even though the Bo tried in vain to sound authoritative.

'My name is James D. Smith. Folks just call me JD, sir.' He added the respectful 'sir', and he observed that it made the two men happy, and threw them even further off guard.

Of course some of the old hobos had long ago told him never to give his real name in such a situation.

'What you got that getar for, boy, can you play it?' the big guy asked.

'Yeah, sure I can play a little,' was Delta's reply. He deliberately dropped the 'sir' as a test of his position.

'Now you look a heah, boy, just cause we are still letting you ride in this heah box car with us, don't mean that suddenly we are equals. Now it's best that you remember your place. Now I'm real sure what you meant to say was "Yes sir" I can play a little. Am I right, boy?' The big guy yelled at Delta, putting as much menace in his voice as he could muster.

'Yessa boss! Y'll are sho right, that's what I rightly meant to say.'

'That's a whole lot better, it's good that we understand each other. Now boy can you sing "Dixie" or something real good?' the man with the squeaky voice said.

'No, we ain't got no time for no singing. Listen, boy, you give us your money, your getar, or your worthless life. It's just that plain, you hear me?' The big guy yelled above the noise of the train.

Now old Delta knew he was out of time, seeing as how the two Bos were getting nasty. So he got to his feet and began to fumble in his pockets as if he was digging out his few meagre coins. The freight train's whistle blew a long low moan as it approached an unguarded railroad crossing.

Some years before he was killed, Buddy gave Delta an old bone-handled razor, and took the time to instruct him in its proper use, both to shave with, and to discourage anyone who was bent on doing him bodily harm. The time was upon him to use it, and not for shaving.

In the meantime, the big hobo pulled an old rusty hog leg that looked like a Smith and Wesson 38. He pointed the old pistol right at Delta's head, and his face suddenly took on the look of a grinning Death's head.

Delta rolled his eyes, and appeared scared to death. Just like he was expected to do. The big guy holding the pistol grinned in satisfaction, and relaxed, thinking that Delta was just another scared nigger.

Now that was about the same time that old Delta pulled his Equaliser and flipped it into the proper fighting position, and all in one smooth fluid motion. At the same instant he moved on the man with the gun, 'cause that man offered him the most threat.

The big guy holding the gun didn't feel no pain, or even know that he was cut, grievously cut. Oh to be sure, he heard the Song of Death the old bone-handled razor sang to him as it cut him, long, deep, wide, and continuously.

The old 38 fell to the floor as the second Bo, upon seeing the work done on his pal, promptly wet his dirty pants.

What took place in the close confines of that end of the box car was way beyond the comprehension of the two hobos. The smell of fresh bloody human faeces, and urine mixed with a generous amount of just plain old fear, pervaded the normal smells of the box car.

Delta didn't want to kill either of the two hobos. He did want to teach them a lesson, a lesson they would always remember, even if they lived to reach a hundred and fifty years of age.

And the next black man they met they wouldn't dare call him Boy.

So he cut them in places that would be painful but not fatal, a gift of life they surely would not have extended to him. While he worked on the big Bo, the little Bo stood frozen in place with abject fear. Then Delta started on him. While working on the two, he repeated over and over, 'Don't call me boy!'

The two Bos didn't even try to fight back, they were too busy trying to save their collective asses. And maybe, just maybe, they came to understand the real intentions of the words: 'We hold these truths to be self-evident, that all Men are created equal.'

Both men took the only option open to them. They jumped, screaming in pain and frustration as they disappeared out the door. Delta wiped his trusty Equaliser and put it back in his pocket.

He made a quick visual inspection of the car to ensure his work was not witnessed, and he was alone, then he threw the personal belongings of the two unfortunates out the door. The 38 was unloaded and the cartridges plus the pistol followed the two pouches out.

He knew better than to keep the old pistol, to be caught with it would certainly be an invitation to disaster. After that he sat back down and was taking stock of his position when he realised too late that the train was slowing down for the built-up areas as it was nearing the yards of New Orleans.

It was far too late for him to jump. The freight was within the outer limits of the Yards, and there was already a lot of yard dicks with lanterns and billy clubs at the ready, just waiting for some poor soul to make the mistake of showing himself.

Perhaps he could outrun them if he didn't have his guitar, and to leave it was strictly out of the question. Besides, the groups of armed men were closely watching the freight he was riding, sort of like a welcoming committee, he didn't stand a chance, it was too late to jump. He was trapped.

His only real ally was the darkness, and that would soon give way to the coming light of the early morning. On top of that, as the train slowed down even more, he could see some of the more zealous or bloodthirsty groups already crawling all over the train. Oh what to do, was it his time to suffer? His thoughts ran to the sickening sight of BC lying there dying on the kitchen table.

If he was caught in that box car with a still bloody straight razor, blood on his hands and on the floor, he would be history. They would put him 'under' the Louisiana State Pen. And that's a sad fact.

The freight train slowed down even more, and he could hear the voices of those in charge as they shouted orders to the gathering mobs.

The train screeched to a complete halt, coming to a stop in an open area that was void of any other trains, or standing box cars. They were on both sides, and some coming from the rear and some from the front, or engine. They were checking each car. Some were even walking on top. Looked like there was a whole army heading directly for him.

'The rubber was on the road.'

Old Delta tried very hard not to panic. Sure that wasn't the first tight spot he was ever in. On the other hand, he had to admit it was right up front to be the tightest. In his mind he heard Buddy talk about the Louisiana Penal System, and say it was even below the standards of Devils Island. Specially if you were black.

Crouching there by the hole in the wall, he thought it was all over, 'cept the tears and the pain. He started to push his guitar through the hole, follow it, and run for it, knowing he wouldn't get thirty feet away before a bullet brought him down. Maybe a bullet in the back would be a more dignified way to go. He started to stick the bottom portion of Fanny Mae through the hole when a clear voice spoke to him.

'Git yourself together, boy! Use the Black Cat's Bone there in your

37

juju bag around your neck. Son, that's all you have left.' Jessie's clear voice spoke to him from across time and space. Brought to him through the eternal powers of a true Mother's Love...

Moving quickly, and with no wasted motion, he hid his guitar under the rubbish. Then he undid the draw string on his juju bag which hung around his neck.

The sounds of the mob grew closer and closer.

Quickly, he located that special small bleached-white bone, from the other things that were in his juju, or mojo bag. He placed the bone into his mouth, redid the string securing the bag and replaced the little bag under his shirt.

Just between you and me, old Delta was more than a little bit nervous, and uncertain about his ability to remember the words of the spell that would provide him with the sacred cloak of invisibility. The incantation was taught to him by Mama Zula when she gave and explained the contents of the little bag to him. But considering the pressure he was under, his mind wasn't working full out.

Two of the groups of armed white men approached the car he was in, one group on the right side and one on the other. He could not only hear them, he could see them through the slats and the hole in the wall. Some of the men were railroad/yard detectives, and some of them were just local red necks with nothing better to do than hunt human beings.

To those men it was like a coon hunt, and he was the treed coon. They were there for the fun of killing a nigger, nothing more.

Delta got an unscheduled relief period when, off to the right side of the car, he could hear the heart-breaking cries of a poor unfortunate black man caught by the mob. The man was crying and begging for his life, which was already forfeit.

The group by his car paused to hear what was going on. They rejoiced in the pitiful cries of the poor man being beating to death, and added their voices to the rabid madness of the mob killing the downed man. Above the baying of the dogs, the cries of the poor man, and the sounds of the tormentors, he could actually hear the dull thuds of the blows raining down on the man, and sapping away his life. A life force they didn't have the power to give him, and it was such a shame, they did have the power to take it away.

Sweet Jesus, they were beating the poor man to death, and Delta was next.

Delta was really scared, and he knew the feeling of a trapped animal. He could see, hear, and feel the moment when the groups of men near the car he stood in decided to proceed with their search. He was next.

Old Delta was clean out of time. 'It's now or never,' he said aloud to himself.

He moved to stand in the corner near the hole in the wall. Then, he stood erect with his feet close together and his arms folded across his chest, the left arm first and the fingers of each hand touching his collar bones. The position of his arms and hands was similar to the same position the arms and hands are placed in an ancient Egyptian mummy.

He began the Ancient Incantation as taught him by Mama Zula:

Gods of my sacred and honoured ancestors, yesterday and today, hear my voice and come take me away.

Make me as the wind, so that I may pass before the hateful eyes of my enemies and be unseen.

Up to the sky, and down to the green, I can no longer be seen.

He held his lips tightly closed, and breathed only through his nose. The Black Cat's Bone was held between his inner lip and gum, snuff-dipper fashion.

He could see them, but they couldn't see him ...

Oh, now the dogs could see him, but the magic of the Black Cat's Bone told the dogs that Delta was one of them, and as such he posed no threat. They totally accepted old Delta as just another dog, one of their group.

Two men actually jumped up into the box car, and went over the inside with the proverbial fine tooth comb. They did not see Delta Sonny or find his guitar. Even though he stood right there among them in plain view. Their lanterns lit up the inside of the car like the light of day. Still they could not see the man standing before them.

The ancient and sacred juju of the Black Cat's Bone held true ...

39

Delta was invisible to the human eye. He was like the wind, and if it wasn't for his guitar it was possible for him to jump down from the freight car and walk off into the night.

All that, right under the very noses of the mob, and no one would have seen him. Thus was the power of the sacred Black Cat's Bone.

'It's empty. Y'all let's move on to see if we can catch any one else before it's too late. Let's just lock the doors and go on to the next car,' one of the railroad dicks yelled to the men around the car. When he spoke he was looking straight at the place where Delta was standing very still and unmoving. The man looked right through him.

The groups of men moved on down the line of freight cars, and old Delta was saved. Thanks to his Black Cat's Bone.

Chapter 6

Minstrel

Nobody knows the trouble I've seen,
Nobody knows but Jesus.
Sometimes I'm up Sometimes I'm down,
Glory Hallelujah!

Delta remained in the sacred position of the dead, until the mob dispersed. Perhaps they went off in search of another black life to take, or to brag about how many men they caught and murdered that morning.

Only when he was sure the danger was past, and he heard and felt the bump as the jump locomotive hooked up to the cars to put them in their assigned places, did he break concentration.

Only then did he say aloud the Bantu incantation which would release the spell of the Black Cat's Bone, and to that incantation he added his plea to Osiris, the ancient Egyptian god whose annual death and resurrection personified the self-renewing vitality of life.

The incantation to end the spell had to end with the words:

'From Life – to Death – to Life.'

Mama Zula had stressed that he must say those exact words, and only after beseeching Ancient Osiris. If the spell was tried in any other way, or order, the results would be instant destruction.

41

That's why those few who dabbled in the occult without proper credentials often left only a burned spot to testify that they once existed.

When he whispered the last sacred words, there was a momentary shimmering of the natural light and air within the confines of the box car. After that phenomenal occurrence all things were returned to normal. And Delta Sonny stood revealed.

He removed the life-saving small bone from his mouth, and after thanking the African gods, and Osiris, he held the bone in the palm of his left hand and rubbed it in a circular motion, using the longest finger of his right hand.

Delta replaced the small Black Cat's Bone back into his juju bag with a lot more respect than he had for it when he took it out. Once the bag was secured and back in its regular place hanging from the thin thong around his neck, he took Fanny Mae, his guitar, from its place of concealment, and prepared to split the scene.

When he was ready, he slowly thrust his head through the opening in the wall to check if the coast was clear. There was no one in sight; he jumped and moved off towards the nearest out-of-the-way portion of the yards

The first light of the new day was well upon him as he made his way to the roadway and started walking toward that portion of New Orleans that Mama Zula told him to go.

Later that morning, he finally arrived at the street and address she gave him. The fact that Mama Zula sent him was enough. He was shown to a nice bedroom and given the necessary things to freshen up, after which he was treated to a wonderful New Orleans breakfast.

After eating his fill, he did not forget to properly thank his benefactor, who was a very lovely tiny white-haired woman. The fact that she was in the same profession as Mama Zula was quite evident. She told him they were having gumbo and rice for supper, in his honour.

She also told him about the incident in the railroad yards, and that the man they beat 'was indeed dead, but his soul was at peace in the kingdom across the river'. She had a way about her that made him so much at home, and feel like Jessie was with him.

The room was small and clean, the bed comfortable, and old Delta slept for almost two days. Oh, he didn't sleep past the gumbo, just got up, ate and went right back to calling hogs.

When he finally woke up, the nice lady spent some time talking to him. She told him that Blind Lemon once slept in the same room. She went on to give the names of some of the great Bluesmen who once came to her house; among the many names were Lonnie Johnson, Leadbelly, O Red, Robert Johnson, and Son House, to name only a few.

Mama Le Beaux was quite a woman, and had been around for a long time.

She told him where the best places were to play, and he decided to wait till the late evening before he went out for the first time.

> My Lord didn't come in the morning or even in the heat of
>   the day.
> My Lord done come in the evening so he could drive old
>   Satan away...
> Oh Lord I want two wings to veil my face
> Oh Lord I want two wings to fly away so the world can't do
>   me no harm.

Shortly before dark, Delta was down on Basin Street where a lot of people meet. He picked a corner that looked good; Mama Le Beaux said that Charlie Patton once played that same corner. His little flat board was in place on the sidewalk, and his heart and soul was full of the Mississippi delta, the birthplace of the Blues as he knew them.

'I got me a stone pony,' he began to play and sing, to pick and moan. Oh, I tell you he just had that old delta feeling and it flowed right on into his voice, guitar and harp.

Why, before he was halfway through 'Hurry down Sunshine', already a crowd was gathered to hear him. There were already a few coins in his old black hat turned upside down for the purpose of receiving alms or what ever you want to call it.

He felt good, it was like Buddy and Sonny Boy were playing back up for him. Blind Lemon told him to play 'Black Snake Moan'. It was always a crowd pleaser for him when he played the streets of Dallas. So old Delta began:

> Oh, I ain't got no mama now, oh I ain't got no mama now.
> She told me late last night, you don't need no mama no how.
> Umm, black snake crawling in my room,
> And some pretty mama had better come and get this snake soon.
> Oh, that must been a bed bug you know a chinch can't bite that hard.

The crowd grew and grew as he played and sang the Blues like he never sang before, and he did it in the proud old tradition of such legends as Charlie Patton, Blind Lemon, Peetie Wheatstraw, Blind Willie McTell and Robert Johnson.

His old white shirt was plastered to his body with his sweat, and the sweat from his brow ran down and burned his eyes. But that was nothing to the burning of the Blues way down in his soul. The bitter sweet melodies flowed from him like the cool waters of a mountain stream, like the muddy waters of the mighty Mississippi.

During the next few weeks he worked central New Orleans, staying always on the move and trying very hard not to work the same spot twice. From South Rampart, the corners of St Louis Cemetery, Jackson Square, Front Street, and on down to Poydras Wharf, Delta played and sang the Mississippi Blues like never before. And he was pleased beyond words when he began to hear people call his name, and say 'Delta Sonny, please play for us.'

He played the light and the dark spots, the hot and the cold spots, two funerals and a Cajun jamboree. Sometimes he played for only one person, sometimes he played for great crowds, and sometimes he played alone.

But one thing for sure, when and wherever he played and sang, he did it with all the heart he could muster. He always felt that the spirits of the old Bluesmen gone on before him were always there watching and listening to him, so he had to do his very best, always.

He swore that he would do it that way right up till the time he crossed the Big River, and he sure hoped the ferry master would allow him to take Fanny Mae on with him.

Now old Delta travelled all over the city playing and singing the Blues, when and wherever he stopped. Some folks put money in his hat, and sometimes they put fruit, candy, peanuts/goobers, or even cigarettes. Course when he got things like that he was playing for folks who just didn't have any money, but still they wanted to give him something, and Delta always took the time to say 'Thanks'. Even if the gift was only a penny or a peanut.

Frankly, he sang even harder for those folks, 'cause they were really 'his folks' a lot more than those who had made it.

He travelled as far as Beaumont, Texas, Lake Charles, Baton Rouge, New Iberia, and Shreveport, Louisiana, not to mention all those little places in-between. Back again in Mississippi he played Gulfport, Biloxi, Pascagoula and on up to Vicksburg.

All that time old Delta played and sang the Blues like no one ever did before him.

You know, somewhere along the way, the true Bluesman that was Delta Sonny came on out and was heard, as he worked his way back on up towards Belzoni and his mother, Miss Jessie Washington. Sho Nuf!

Chapter 7

Christmas in November

Jessie was so happy to see him. Words of how well he did throughout the south land had already preceded him. Folks was comparing his style of Blues to that of one of the old time greats, and his harp was second only to Sonny Boy himself.

Even though folks didn't have access to telephones, and most folks couldn't even read or write, their grapevine was one of the best in the country, in the world for that matter. And Jessie was kept abreast of his progress by that very same grapevine.

It was after lay-by time, and somewhere around late November, that she knew deep down in her heart, and through the Old Ways from Mother Africa that for sure her boy was on his way home.

Matter of fact, the very same day that he got home, she had already fixed his favourite winter meal, and had it still warm and waiting for him. She prepared fresh crackling bread with crowder peas, cooked on down low with smoked and fresh meat skins. There were sweet potato pies and piping hot sassafras tea. Of course, the pies were cooked the day before and allowed to set over night, so by the time he got home they were just right. They were ready to be enjoyed, along with a cold glass of butter milk.

Soon as everything was ready, she went out on the front porch to wait.

Sure enough, when she looked up, he was turning off the road and just coming past the mail box. On top of that he was just loaded down with packages, and of course he was carrying Fanny Mae, his guitar, like always.

Old Rattler was already half way to him and pulling full out. Jessie laughed and said out loud, 'My, my! That old dog better slow down, he ain't run so hard in a long time. He's going to mess around and pass out from sheer exhaustion.'

Delta only slowed down to talk to his old friend, he couldn't pet him 'cause he didn't want to put his packages on the damp ground. He came on to the house and the waiting arms of his mother.

Oh I tell you it was so good for her to hold close to her all that she had left in the world. She couldn't and didn't try to hold back the tears of joy that filled her heart. After hugging each other over and over again, they just stood there looking, eye to eye.

> If I could only hear my mother pray again,
> If I could hear her tender voice again.
> Oh how proud I would be,
> It would mean so much to me.
> If I could hear my dear mother pray again.

Yes, old Delta was crying too. They were both happy and sad, 'cause you see, it was brought right on back to them that old death had taken a terrible toll on the Washington family. Delta tried to push away the sadness.

'Look here, Mama, what I brought specially for you.' She helped him to take the packages into the house, and old Rattler came right along, his tail wagging like all get out.

A pair of pink house shoes, a Sunday go-to-meeting dress, along with a nice hat with pretty things on it. Some fancy women underthings, handkerchiefs and a beautiful shiny black pair of shoes, all the way from New Orleans. Plus some other things, along with a real leather pocketbook full of money. Not coins, but real paper money, United States green back dollars.

Oh! It was just like Christmas, the best Christmas Jessie had ever had. Christmas in November. She cried so much she couldn't see, and couldn't stop saying over, and over again, 'Thank the good Lord...'

While Delta ate his wonderful meal, he told her about the incident in the railroad yards of New Orleans, and how he had used the Black Cat's Bone given to him by Mama Zula. He told her about some of the places he travelled to, and about the wonderful people he met along the way. During that time she sat quietly and listened to what her son had to tell her, it was like she had visited all those places too. Fact was, she had only been as far away from Belzoni as Jackson, and that was only for one time.

After they finished eating, she tried on all her wonderful once-in-a-lifetime gifts. Everything fit. Except the shoes, they were a little too tight. But she didn't let on about it.

Later, they sat by a small fire built to provide comfort more than heat, and they talked about Yesterday, and their loved ones gone on across the River. Delta had already stopped by Shady Grove, to pay his respects to his family lying there in the cemetery.

He reflected on the fact that they were all victims of the times, and being born black. He promised them that he would do all that he could to take good care of his mother.

He could see that Jessie had lost some weight, and the usual bright fire in her soft brown eyes was noticeably no longer so bright and full of life.

'Mama, let me take you to Chicago. There you can have a better life for yourself, a whole lot better than sitting here in this old shack by yourself, and no one to keep you company.'

'Why, Son, I surely do thank you so much for that wonderful offer. But you see, Son, here on Lightcap's is my home. It's the only home I know an' I guess it's the only home that I want to know. Son, I'm country. The Mississippi delta is me, and I'm the delta. Plain an' simple.'

'Why, I wouldn't know how to get along way up there in the big Windy City. I hear it gets pretty cold, and there is no place to raise a few chicken or a nice garden. Let's face it, I couldn't live like that. Besides, I know you remember Percy Williams. They use to live across the highway, and near the woods in the place with the new roof. He took you to play with him at a Christmas jook, which was your last Christmas home. I know you haven't forgotten, 'cause y'll had to run for your lives.

'Well, Son, sometimes ago Percy came and asked me if we could live together, and I said OK. So I'm not really here all alone. I knew you were coming sometimes today, so I asked him to wait till round supper time before he came home. That way I could have the time to talk to you first. That way there will be no hard feelings about him being here. Son, he is real good to me.'

'No, Ma'am, I surely don't have no problems with Percy living with you. Fact is I'm glad that you got someone, and you ain't alone. Does he really treat you OK? Now I know old Percy is given to drinking, whenever he can get a-hold of something...'

'Son, it's the truth, he really is good to me, we haven't had a mean word between us since he's been here. Even though sometimes he stopped off and had a few before coming home, he still treated me better than anyone ever did before. He works at the gin, and we also raised a little cotton, so we're doing pretty well. He even offered to take me to live in Jackson or Brookhaven but I said here was where I wanted to be.'

Shortly before dark, Percy came home, and they were very happy together. Just like a real family. Delta had a full pint of sealed whisky, so it wasn't long before he and Percy was in it. Of course that led to the point that they started to sing and play: 'I got love for my baby, and my baby got love for me', 'Must I holler or must I shake em on down', 'I'm a poor boy long way from home'.

Oh, they were getting on down when there was a knock on the front door. 'Come on in!' Jessie yelled over the music. Her nearest neighbours, Sam and Millie Peters, were passing by, heard the music and stopped in.

Course Jessie was happy, their coming made it just right for a party. So she and Millie went into the kitchen to see what they could come up with. Sam took Jessie's washboard and joined Percy and Delta. After that they went on back. They played and sang happy Blues and sad Blues, train Blues, working Blues, who did what to who Blues, and going to Chicago Blues.

Jessie had almost half a gallon of White Lightning stuck away so she broke it out. Boy, I tell you, that stuff was strong enough to go wild cat hunting with a tooth pick. They had to mix it with lots of water and still when it went down it curled their hair. She didn't have to worry about them drinking it all, no one had the intestinal fortitude.

Oh, they broke 'em on down till first light. Millie Peters sang a few songs, she surely did have a nice singing voice, and a whole lot of soul. Oh, that girl had the voice quality and could sing so much like the Empress of the Blues, Miss Bessie Smith.

But you know, when she sang 'Shake it Down' and 'Pratt City Blues', she could slide her voice and sound so much like the Great Lillian Glinn. Some folks said that Lillian wasn't from the delta, but maybe from Texas or Louisiana.

Oh they had a great time, even Jessie joined in the singing, she was so happy to welcome her son home. And, to hear him sing and play, plus his harp had mellowed out, brought on by his playing with the great Sonny Boy, on top of his many years with his Grandpa Buddy Washington.

So he wasn't a Baptist preacher, and preaching the word of God. On the other hand, you could say that he was preaching the Blues, and carrying the word to the people. After all, the real Blues was truly the heritage of the black people, their birthright, and to preach that birthright to them was surely like being on a mission from the African gods of the beginning.

She smiled, as she thought to herself that her son, Roosevelt Lincoln Washington, RW, or Delta Sonny, was a Bluesman in his own right.

Once the new day was there, they carried on with what they had to do. After the chores, they caught a few winks. Then they restarted the day, and along about three or four o'clock Jessie and Delta went to see Mama Zula, and she insisted that they break bread with her.

Fresh pork fried golden brown, wild rice with lots of special herbs, candied yams, and thick skillet bread, all washed down with strong chicory coffee was their treat.

After they ate, Mama Zula took Delta's juju bag and threw it into the fire. She intoned an unearthly sounding chant that was like nothing Jessie or Delta had ever heard.

It all started when, without any indication of what she was about to do, she simply reached inside his collar, grabbed the leather thong, cut it with a knife they didn't see before that instant and threw it in the fire.

As she chanted her mystic incantation, smoke billowed from the burning juju bag and came into the living room. The smoke took on the form of dancing African warriors, and the dancers danced around the living. Delta was scared to death. He had heard, but not seen. The colour of the smoke was definitely red.

Mama Zula sadly shook her white head. The red smoke was a bad omen for Delta.

She decided not to tell Delta or his mother what she saw coming, or the meaning of the sacred red smoke issuing from the burning juju bag. Of course the dancing ebony warriors told her that at least Delta would not forfeit his life. He would live through the tribulations, and the great suffering that he would bring on himself.

No! Old Delta would have to sleep in the bed he would make, and when he got up on the other side of the bed he would be a better man. That was the price the gods would exact.

No one knew how old Mama Zula was; everyone knew she was a witch, a sorceress, or/and a hoodoo woman. Folks, both black and white, came to see her from as far away as New York. When she couldn't help them, and if she was asked to recommend someone else, in her own words, she would say, 'There is one who taught me all that I know, one who can walk on the wind, and climb the ladders of time, "she that is" is the bridge between here and there. But I cannot send you to her, even though she is not too far from here. If she is to help you, she will contact you, and not you her. There is no other way.'

Mama Zula didn't pick no cotton, she did plant corn, and how long she lived on Lightcap's was unknown, even to the big boss man himself. The only time he came to see her was when he had a problem, or needed a magic potion or mojo bag for himself.

She lived all alone way down in the bottom and surrounded by the woods and a lot of pecan trees. Folks said that she could talk to the animals and that most of her friends were the forest creatures who were always around her house day or night. They said it was

51

impossible to approach her house without her knowing you were coming. The animals told her everything.

There was the story which said that one night there were six Ku-Klux-Klansmen who decided to go to her house and burn a cross in her front yard, 'Cause she was too Uppity'.

Well the six Klansmen rode up to her front yard that night, and thinking falsely that she wasn't aware of their approach, or their intentions. Once they were there, their leader pulled his gun and shot a hole in her front door.

To scare the Hell out of her, and teach her a lesson. Also to announce their arrival.

Those old boys was asking for it.

The rest of the story was told by the Klansmen who were unfortunate and fool enough to call Mama Zula out.

When the leader put the shot through her door, she suddenly appeared, standing right there on her front porch before them, and they didn't see her coming. Well, they said that Mama Zula offered to let them turn around and get out of there. Soon as they 'fixed the hole in her front door'.

Even though they wore their hoods to cover their cowardly faces, Mama Zula called each man by his correct name. But because she was a lone black woman, and they were six big strong white men, they got real mad and decided to 'fix her wagon, permanently'. Which was a very bad decision.

She stood there smiling at them, and clicking her tongue. They said she never raised her voice at them, or appeared angry. On a signal from the leader, two of the white-sheeted men got down from their horses and began to erect the cross which was wrapped in kerosene-soaked rags. At that same time the other men got off their horses and went to grab hold of her.

The leader reached out to grab her arm. And if he was living today you would easily recognise him by his snow-white hair, and the fact that he was never able again to lower his right arm ...

Three of the Klansmen swore to the pastor of their church that 'a great big wild cat jumped out from behind where the old woman was standing, and that cat was the meanest son-of-a-bitch they ever had the misfortune of meeting.'

The wild cat flew into them and tore out ragged patches of human flesh and scalp, some with hair still attached. Ripped pieces of white bed sheets rained down like it was snowing. Blood, shit, and gore was all over the front yard.

They said that old cat fully lived up to his name. He tore into the Klansmen with a vengeance. He was on them like stink on cat shit, broke out on them like a bad case of poison ivy. He worked on all of them at the same time. They bellowed and screamed in terrible pain. Finally one of the smartest of the six figured out that their only salvation was in the hands of the little old woman who was standing quietly and watching the show.

'Call him off! Please ma'am, call him off.' By that time they were almost naked, and covered with blood. The horses were not afraid of the wild cat, and moved casually off to nibble the grass. One of the downed men was clearly heard to call his mama.

The torches they brought and long since dropped to the ground still burned brightly and cast the light which illuminated the stage and scene of the both tragic and comic opera.

She could see all their faces cast in terror, and particularly the face of the good old boy grovelling on the ground and calling his mama. She didn't want him to die of a heart attack and further clutter up her front yard.

On the other hand, if she didn't call that old cat off they might all die from Wildcatitis.

She called the cat off with a single word; he came immediately to sit by the tip of her apron, and began to clean the blood off his long sharp claws. She thought about letting him kill the bastards, but decided against it, too much of a problem getting rid of the bodies.

She knew they were all messed up and in great pain, still she made them clean up her front yard, and fix the bullet hole in her front door. They helped their leader up on his horse, with his right arm and hand sticking up in the air. His mind was scrambled and his trousers was full. All in all, he stunk something awful.

Years later when the leader died, the undertaker had to break his arm to get him in the casket.

Of course it was some time passed before they told anyone what really happened that night. Their first lie was that they came across a 'whole bunch of wild cats'. But it was always funny they could never get their story together, and the leader never spoke again after that night.

Course the good folks noticed that whenever they mentioned Mama Zula they all called her 'Mother Zula', except the leader; when he heard her name, he promptly peed his pants. Every time he did the same thing.

After that no one ever bothered Mama Zula again.

The five remaining Klansmen resigned from the organisation, and wouldn't go within five miles of Mama Zula's place.

It's said that three of the four still functioning Klansmen actually submitted applications to join the National Association for the Advancement of Coloured People (NAACP).

Chapter 8

C C Rider

Even to that very same day, what was left of the cross the Klan brought to burn in Mama Zula's front yard was still lying there. The bullet hole shot in her front door could still be seen. All that was mute testimony to what happened that night long ago.

Well, anyway, Mama Zula did give Delta a replacement juju bag. However, the contents of that bag didn't include a Black Cat's Bone. She gave him specific instructions that he was never to remove the bag from around his neck.

'If it should come off by accident you must put it back on as soon as you can. You can remove it to take a bath, or if absolutely necessary you can put it in your pocket for a short time. However, if someone else should remove it, or you take it off and the cock crows twice while you have it off, then the mojo of the bag will return back here to me, where it will stay.'

'Delta, you must avoid going to Clarksdale at all cost. I tell you true, if you should go to Clarksdale old Trouble is going to jump on your back and ride you for three years, all the way right up to the gates of hell.

'Son, if you don't do exactly like I'm telling you, the time will come that you will sleep with the devil, a devil with six toes on one foot.'

He let her place the new juju bag around his neck, and when she was finished, he thanked her and gave her his word in the presence of his mother, that he would do just like she said. He promised never to allow anyone to remove his bag, and that he would definitely not go to Clarksdale, under any circumstances.

Mama Zula looked at him and smiled a sad smile, sort of like she already knew what was going to be. The worm was going to eat the bird...

Delta spent a little over a week with his mother and Percy, until the long lonesome call of the six-fifteen told him it was time for him to move on down that lonesome road.

It was time for him to reach up and grab iron.

He jumped off the freight just north of Greenville, and made his way back, that was an old hobo's trick Buddy told him about. There was two other guys working the streets, so he moved on to Winona, and on up to Tupelo. Meridian and Hattiesburg were very good to him, so much so, he hated to leave, but before long it was time for him to slide on over to Natchez.

Birmingham, Alabama, was also very nice to him. He met an old girl who put him up for the whole time he was there, but she wanted him to marry her, and that wasn't in the cards. So he moved on into Georgia for a while.

He was down in Columbus and playing for the soldier boys stationed at Fort Benning when he got the word that Sonny Boy, Lightning, and Old JD were going to be in Jackson for something big. So he caught him a Dog and pulled on into Jackson town.

He found Sonny Boy and Lightning playing at Mancy's, and he got a room with JD in a private home on Church Street not too far from Smith Robertson School. The next day they came together at the Big Apple on Ferris Street to plan what they were going to do.

There was a professor at Piney Woods who wanted them to play for a special occasion. Something about where the Blues came from, and they would play for the students and faculty.

It would be almost like a concert, and Delta was happy for the chance to play, that would be his first time playing for such an audience. Plus there would also be the grand opportunity for him to meet some of the other Bluesmen of that time.

The hall, or auditorium, they played was very nice, and the crowd was even nicer and anxious to hear what they had to offer. Frankly, Delta couldn't help but feel kind of out of place, and being there reminded him that he couldn't read or write well.

Before they went on, there was a guy who played hell out of the piano, and beat out so much boogie woogie that he had them dancing all over the place.

Howling Wolf and a little guy from Louisiana came late but they were able to get on the pay roll. While he was waiting his turn to go on, he took a good look around, and discovered there were some real legends there waiting their turn to play.

After old Sam finished playing, Delta could understand why everyone called Sam Hopkins 'Lightning'. Oh he was fast, and to top it off, he was just plain old good.

When it was finally Delta's turn he decided to start off with 'Devil in the Woodshed'. Then he did 'Black Snake Moan', and ended with a number from Blind Willie McTell, which was 'Travelling Blues'.

Later he and Sonny Boy did 'Good Evening Little Schoolgirl'. Oh, I tell you, they brought the house down. Everyone was ready when Howling Wolf did 'Little Red Rooster', and 'Highway 49'. By that time the joint was rocking, and everyone had fun well on into the night.

She was standing by one of the open side doors and trying to catch a breath of fresh air, while she was talking to another girl. Delta couldn't take his eyes off her. In all his young life she was truly the most beautiful woman he ever saw.

When she finally looked at him and smiled, his legs turned to rubber and his heart tried to jump out of his chest. He was overcome like a schoolboy on his first crush. But Delta was too old for that, or was he?

Her name was Jewel, and within the first few minutes of their being close together, she opened his nose so wide that if it would rain, old Delta would surely drown.

Jewel was high yeller, which was in vogue at that time. And that child had a body that would make a preacher lay his Bible down, and a dead man smile. She had pretty soft hair, light brown eyes, and her legs should have been insured, and declared a national treasure.

When the gig was over, Jewel took Delta home, threw him in her big brass bed, and rocked him till his face turned cherry red.

'You got to get rid of that stinking old hoodoo, or asafetida bag you got around your neck. If you want me again, that damn old bag has got to go first! This is the 1940s and that old superstitious bullshit went out with slavery,' she scolded him.

Then she snatched the little bag from around his neck and ran from the bedroom.

He sat naked in the bed, and not fully comprehending what was happening. That is till he heard the toilet flush, and then he knew she had pulled the chain on his juju bag. It was history, and on its way to the local sewage distillery.

Poor old Delta was drunk from the sheer aftermath of her. His mind was in a purple cloud, and not functioning properly, if it was functioning at all.

It's a known fact that when a man has a strong sexual desire for a woman, often the thinking part of his brain goes out to lunch. In other words he stops thinking.

That was the condition old Delta found himself in.

Too late, he realised the enormity of what was going down. Cold chills racked his body and the desire for more sex faded. But he was soon overcome by stupidity, when he said to himself, 'Oh well, she's right, it's only a lot of superstitious shit, and it was beginning to stink like hell.' Still, he couldn't forget standing there in that box car right before the eyes of at least ten men, and they couldn't see him. The Black Cat's Bone really did work.

When they finally couldn't go no more, and sleep or talk was all that was left, she told him, 'You know, baby, I'm going to Chicago to live. I already have an apartment on Warren Boulevard, and a decent job. I'm tired of being a nobody nigger woman, so I'm getting the hell out of old Jim Crow's homeland. A real good friend of mine let me have his car to drive up with. Sugar, why don't you come on and go with me? There is a whole lot more of what I just gave you waiting to be had.

'Baby, you are good, you sure can play and sing the Blues, and I promise, you can sure do better in the Windy City. Besides, Muddy and Jimmy are both friends of mine, and if I ask them to do something for you they will, maybe even let you record with them. Yeah, that's it, if you come with me, I'll get you into a recording studio. You know I helped set up the show at Piney Woods.

'Oh, I'm leaving tomorrow, and if you come with me I have only one short stop on the way. I promised Mother that I would stop by to see her and Dad on the way up. It's right on our way. Have you ever been to Clarksdale?'

She put her arms around him, and crushed her ample breast against his chest, as her soft lips blew the rest of what sense he may have had left, right out the window.

Oh, she really did take unfair advantage of that poor fool, 'cause he agreed to whatever she had to say. Ain't it funny how some folk get the term 'weaker sex' confused?

Early that Saturday morning they packed her car and took off for Clarksdale, Mississippi. Old Delta was doing exactly what Mama Zula told him not to do.

When they arrived at her parents' house, and after the introductions, he was well accepted by both her mother and father. The house was very nice and well kept. Both the house and street were an example of the emerging, 'educated and fair-the-well Negroes in the wartime South'. Even in his poor state of mind, he could tell that her mother and father were used to the pain of her bringing different men home, and on a recurring basis.

There was a telephone in the house and Jewel right away rushed to call 'Charles'. 'Just to let him know I'm here with his car'. They talked for a few minutes, and even though she tried to keep it a secret, old Delta knew when she told Charles that he was with her. Her tone of voice and the expression on her pretty face told the whole story.

She hung up, and disappeared into the kitchen with her Mom.

Charles arrived in less than twenty minutes after the call. He was typical of those coloured folks who had made it. You could smell the bleaching cream above the aroma of his sweet-smelling toilet water. He was dressed like 'them' and carried away with himself. Right away, and soon as he was introduced to Delta, the daggers his eyes threw were unmistable, and if looks could kill, Delta would have died a thousand times over.

The story was that he was in Clarksdale to visit his ailing grandmother, and lent his car to Jewel for the concert, and to drive it back to Chicago. He would return home via train at a later date.

Shortly after Charles arrived, Jewel's parents suddenly came up with some weak excuse that they had to visit a sick friend, a previous engagement they almost forgot. They went away to leave the house to the young folk.

Delta's gut feeling told him that Jewel and Charles were lovers. Why she brought him along wasn't clear at all, unless old Charlie was a wham-bam-thank-you-ma'am kind of lover.

Frankly, that's exactly what he looked like. On the other hand maybe Charlie Boy was a Three Dollar Bill. One thing for sure, he didn't like Delta and Delta sure didn't like him.

From the git go, Charles threw off on Delta. Every chance he took he used that opportunity to point out to Jewel that Delta was country, stupid, and 'just an out-of-work Bum'. Of course, she tried to laugh it all off, and never once came to Delta's defence. After sitting and talking for a while, she asked Delta to 'Please go down to the store on the corner and get her a pack of Lucky Strikes. Charles couldn't go cause he and the owner didn't get along.'

Well, you see, old Delta agreed to go 'cause he just about had it with Charles. Fact was he was very close to breaking out on Charles like a bad case of clap. The little store was way down to the farthest corner of the street, and Delta took his time going and coming so he could cool off.

Upon returning back to the house, he just came on into the living room without knocking and was on his way to the kitchen, when he clearly heard the grunting and groaning. All the sound effects was accompanied with the loud sounds of flesh slapping against naked flesh. His heart sank like the *Titanic*.

They were on her bed, she was buck naked, and Charles had his trousers down around his ankles. While he was in the process of riding her like the Lone Ranger rode Silver. If Charles was funny, he sure as hell didn't look like it then.

C C Rider, see what you have done.
You made me love you,
Now your man done come.

The ache in his heart and loins was excruciating as he stood there in the doorway, held motionless by what he saw, heard, smelled, and painfully felt. For that moment, what was left of his mind was on hold. Of course Charles and Jewel were far too busy to notice that they were being observed...

Something inside Delta snapped, his mind went. He screamed in unbearable pain, rage, and insanity. In that same instant he broke free of the mind-numbing paralysis, and ran over to pull Charles from his commanding position atop the woman that was his first love.

Both she and Charles rained foul curses down on his head for interrupting their love-making, they were almost there. While he struggled with Charles, she attacked him like a wild cat, and dug her long fingernails into his face and neck. The ferocity of her attack caused him to release his hold on her lover, or forfeit his eyes.

He was forced to fight her or lose his eyesight.

While Jewel kept Delta busy, Charles pulled his switchblade knife and the dull light danced on the cold steel blade. He screamed some foul oath about Delta's mother, and lunged to drive the long blade into Delta anywhere he could. Jewel was actually doing her best to hold the man she had made a fool of, for the death thrust.

'No one can make a fool of you. However they sure can bring the fool in you out.'

Old Delta took the only option left open to him, and kicked out with all the strength he could muster in one leg and foot. The kick was good and dead on target. He drove a number ten roach killer right between Charles's legs and destroyed the man's family jewels.

Charles bellowed in pain, and spewed his last meal all over the place as he dropped the knife and grabbed what was left of his ruined manhood. He fell to his knees screaming and puking his guts out.

Jewel also screamed in pure rage, as she dove for the switchblade lying on the floor. Delta was quicker and his rage was out of control.

61

He grabbed the knife first and drove the long blade up to the handle into Charles's chest, and into the heart of the man that he caught riding his first love.

It was all over. He stood over the dead man motionless and in an apparent stupor, seemingly unaware of the endless screeching and screaming of bloody murder by his used-to-be lover.

Somewhere along the line, old Delta clearly looked at Jewel standing there completely naked, and he saw that her right foot was deformed, that foot had SIX TOES...

Time stood still for him. For the very first time, he saw the real woman standing there screaming at him.

She had given him pleasure beyond his wildest dreams, brought him to Clarksdale and tried to hold him until her true lover could take his life.

She had engineered his becoming a murderer, and he did nothing to stop her. He saw her as she truly was. The devil in the body of a beautiful woman.

The words of Mama Zula screamed in his mind: 'Don't go to Clarksdale. If you should go there old Trouble is going to jump on your back and ride you for three years, all the way right up to the gates of hell. And the time will come that you will sleep with the devil, a devil with six toes on one foot.'

> Oh Lord I want two wings to veil my face.
> Oh Lord I want two wings to fly away,
> So the world can't do me no Harm.

Chapter 9

Parchman

The undertakers took Charles's half naked body away, and the local fuzz took Delta. Jewel was still screaming curses at him. Oh, she talked about his mother like she had a tail. She even told the law that 'he murdered poor Charles in cold blood, and in a fit of rage 'cause he caught her and her boyfriend making love'.

She begged the cops to 'Shoot him dead'.

Well, old Delta spent seven days in the local jail, and eleven days on the county farm, from which he was transferred directly to Parchman Penitentiary. Oh, he had a five-minute trial before being sentenced. A big fat man in khaki shirt and trousers wearing a badge, and sitting with his feet up on a worn desk, told Delta he was 'Guilty as Charged, and was going to Parchman'.

One of the guards involved in transferring him to prison was kind enough to tell him that he was going to do 'Three Years, with good behaviour. But, that was subject to change after he got there, and according to how the warden was feeling at the time'.

'And old Trouble will jump up on your back, and ride you for three years . . .' Mama Zula said those words to him before he left Belzoni and home.

He couldn't cry no more, his eyes were dry, red and puffy as he fell in line to began the humiliating and dehumanising prison in-processing.

To be sure, since he was knee high to a boll weevil, he had heard some of the horror stories about old Parchman Farm, and he thought he had some idea about what to expect.

But, I tell you truly. Old Delta wasn't at all prepared for what actually took place. Oh, he thought he was all cried out, but he had a lot more tears to shed.

There is something obscene, and very humiliating to make a man parade buck naked in front of other men, and to hose him down like an old dog.

During that time the world was at war, and the president told the American people that there was nothing to fear but fear itself. The twentieth century was ushering in 'changes' for the country. But sadly enough those changes didn't effect or reach as far down as that place. They were still back in the Dark Ages.

The first night he was there, he witnessed a man being 'chastised'. The man was being whipped, or more correctly said, the man was being beaten.

The poor man was strapped to a rack so his bare back and buttocks were easily accessible to the beater. The strap was a thick leather belt some five or six inches wide, and with round holes about the size of a nickel cut into it. The holes began about four inches from the end, and were placed fairly close together and extending most of the way back to the strong round wood handle.

The man swinging the strap was right at home. Oh, he missed his calling, he would have been right at home as a guard at Buchenwald, Dachau, or just where he was. The red neck's face turned a deep purple, and his eyes glazed over in some indecent ecstasy as he tore the poor guy's back and butt to a pulp.

You see, the force of the strap hitting the soft and yielding flesh, and the holes sucking up the flesh like a giant octopus, was pure cruelty in itself. But there was an added bonus. The holes left small round welts on the skin, and of course continuous beating would cause those welts to finally pop open.

It's very sad to see a man beaten without mercy. Especially if the man being beaten is a black man, and you are a black man, and to top it all off, the beater, the man swinging the strap, is white. To hear the black man scream and cry like a baby, to witness him breaking down, and begging for, 'Mercy, master, mercy!'

Delta was also crying like a little baby child. Hell wasn't 'down there', it was right there in Mississippi. And he was up to his neck in it. A self-inflicted wound.

'Sweet Jesus, if only I had listened to what my mama, and Mama Zula said. If only I was man enough to be a man. I wouldn't be here today,' Delta said to himself, as he cried and cried, in the absence of sleep.

The ghost of the man he killed laughed at him...

They were up way before the first light of day. Flour bread, blackstrap and sorghum molasses, fat back and its grease, plus a tin cup of black coffee was their 'ate-on-the-run' breakfast. After which they shuffled off to where the trucks waited.

Old Delta could no longer walk like a normal man. 'Cause you see by that time he was married up with his first old lady. And she was shackled to his right leg, a large round black ball of iron attached to a chain, and the chain attached to a band of iron fastened around his ankle. Just like a wedding band. Oh, I tell you, sure as hell they were married, and the preacher who married them was the devil himself.

Young Delta Sonny was down on Parchman Farm, where he was issued a new suit of clothes. He wore the black and white stripes of the Forgotten. He was a murderer, he took a man's life. Because of his stupidity, and a no good woman, he was paying his dues.

Mother, don't you worry bout your Son...

The ride to the work site was a reasonably short one. They enjoyed the cool morning air, and the chance to watch the fields of cotton and the fresh green woods pass by. All the time they were under the watchful eyes of the many guards who were all heavily armed. And were known to shoot at the drop of a hat.

The old captain assigned Delta to operate a slip. Now if you don't know what a slip is, let me tell you. It was a big, flat-bottomed metal scoop used to scoop up and move earth. There was a team of mules attached to the front tongue, sort of like a wagon.

The mule teams varied from two to six big strong mules. And it took a real man to run a slip, and run it good.

The gang leader was Big Jim Yancy. And Big Jim was one hell of a man. He stood a full head above all the others. Jim wore his ball and chain like it was made of paper, and had worn it so long that it looked like a natural part of him.

Once you met Big Jim, one thing for sure, you would never forget him. Not just because he was such an imposing figure, or that he never smiled, and his big bass voice could be heard from way off.

But, added to all that was the fact Big Jim was six feet two of pure muscle, black as the ace of spades, and mean enough to break day with a stick.

Old Jim was 'serving three lifetime sentences to run back to back'. Why even his ghost would be doing life in Parchman. Jim had nothing to lose, and nothing to gain.

There was no distinction to him between life and death, or death and life. That was one of the reasons that he was the gang leader.

Please allow me to tell you how old Jim purchased his 'one way ticket to hell, and to old Parchman Pen'.

Now it all came as a direct result of him killing a white man. A white man old Jim caught in the saddle screwing his woman. Oh, it wasn't like the man was raping her, or taking it against her will, no sir!

Fact was, she was giving it to him of her own free will, and that man knew full well that he was screwing Big Jim Yancy's woman.

So Jim killed the man with his bare hands. Broke every bone in the poor fool's body, then he snatched the dead man's head clean off his body and threw it away. Soon as that was done Jim turned his attention to the woman. He crushed her skull like an over-ripe watermelon, and drank her blood.

Then he took off running.

When the Sheriff and his posse finally cornered old Jim down in the woods, they were surely very sorry that they cornered him. They said he destroyed six top-notch blood hounds, broke their necks, or ripped their guts out. Plus he laid up over half of the posse.

Yes. They shot him seven times and he never went down. Any one of the wounds would have brought a normal man down. But they just made old Jim even madder.

He broke out on those good old boys like a bad case of diarrhoea.

66

Until finally, and to their great relief, Jim suddenly stopped destroying them, sat down on a log and said he was 'Tired and didn't want to fight no more . . .'

There wasn't a man there who wasn't glad as hell that old Jim finally stopped kicking their collective asses. A great sigh of relief surged through those still standing, even the remaining dogs stayed a respectable distance away from where he sat. They sure enough did a lot of barking and howling, but they wouldn't go near him.

Well, soon as it sunk into their confused minds that Jim gave up, their cowardice rushed to the front. They were crazed with pain, fear, and the fact that the whole lot of them together couldn't bring Big Jim Yancy down.

He took all they could throw at him and never once left his feet. Now you see, them being the superior and supreme race, and the fact that all of them, plus their guns and dogs failed to bring one black man down was more than they could take, and certainly more than they could allow to become public. Oh no! they didn't want that story to get out.

So they decided to lynch him right there, and keep the story of their total defeat among themselves. They weren't too stupid to know there is some truth in the age old adage that says 'dead men tell no tales'.

Like the pack of hungry wolves they were, as one they sprang upon Jim, tied his hands behind his back, and positioned the hangman's noose (which they always carried with them) around his neck. In only a few minutes, they had Jim tied up, the rope around his neck and on a horse. Through it all, he just smiled at them and offered no resistance whatever.

Then they slapped the horse and the horse ran off. Old Jim was dancing on air. But then the unexpected and unexplained happened. The tree limb broke under his weight, and Jim fell to the ground unharmed except for the rope burn that could still be plainly seen when Delta met him.

Panic reigned supreme among the posse. They didn't know what to do next. They just stood around looking at the bleeding man on the ground and shaking their heads. One man raised his pistol to shoot Jim again in the head, but the man's hands were shaking so much that he couldn't aim the big pistol. He gave up the effort, and dropped the pistol on the ground by his foot.

That's when the sheriff in charge of the posse ran to stand over Jim, and he yelled to the rest of the men these words:

'Boys, now y'all listen to me, and y'all listen to me good. This heah is one hell of a MAN, and I ain't going to let him die this a way, no sir. Now we done shot him, beat him, and lynched him. And as y'all can plainly see, this old boy is still alive. Now that's enough.

'We all know old Billy Bob had the hots for this heah boy's woman for a long time, and even I told Billy that if he just had to have it, to at least take her out in the woods somewhere. But no, he had to go on down to this man's shack, and pile up in his bed with his woman. Let's face it, even though Old Billy was one of us, he was a fool. He knew full well that this old nigger was crazy.

'We're taking Big Jim here back to jail, and we're taking him alive. And I damn well will shoot the first man who tries to prevent me doing what I plan to do. Ya heah that.'

There were no takers to the idea of getting in the sheriff's way. Even the dead man's kinfolk didn't raise no objections. They all agreed to let old Jim Yancy live. Some of them even patched him up so he wouldn't lose too much blood before they got him to a doctor, even if the doctor was a horse doctor.

Well, that's the story on how Big Jim Yancy happened to be serving three life time sentences down on old Parchman Farm. And the story is true, as told by the local sheriff himself.

During the following months Delta ran a slip, worked the end of a pick and shovel, and did whatever job the captain or the guards told him to do. He knew better than to mouth off or do anything to rile them. Ten long hard months he worked his young ass off, and during that time he learned a lot about life, and the real world.

But most of all, he learned a lot about himself.

The Mississippi penal system as directed to blacks was a study in demoniac horror, cruelty, and man's inhumanity to his fellow man. Specially when the man on the receiving end was black. Some of the stories of what happened behind the fences and closed doors during those dark days would put Auschwitz to shame. Sure enough.

Delta didn't have the heart to let his mother know he was in the place where an alarming number of black men always seemed to end up. Some justifiably so, but most of them there because of an unjust legal system, and the people who were supposed to manage that system being even more unjust.

Still, he knew it was only a matter of time before she found out for sure. He knew that the eternal connection of a Mother's love between him and her, had already warned her that he was in trouble. That was understood.

When he thought of her, his eyes always filled up with tears. He was so sorry that he had shamed her by killing a man, and going to prison. The church at Shady Grove and its congregation of her dearest friends was really all that she had. And he had shamed her before them because of a no good woman.

Sure, there were times in conversation with his peers when some of them bragged about how many men they killed. And some of those times he looked upon those men as being 'bad'. But after he was unfortunate enough to take a man's life, he knew for sure that it was nothing to be proud of, and to go around bragging about.

Fact was, old Delta was ashamed of what he did, often he asked the good Lord, and the spirit of the dead man to forgive him. He knew for sure what he did would ride him for the rest of his natural life...

He accepted the bed of nails he made for himself. He couldn't blame the system for his being down on old Parchman Farm. Truth was, he did it to himself. He put himself under the gun. He committed the crime of murder, and the law was making him pay for it. Plain and simple as that.

Delta came to know first hand the cruel system that was his existence, and designed to reduce a man to his lowest form. To reduce him to the point that any similarity between a prisoner and a normal man was purely coincidental.

To do something wrong, or any infraction of the strict rules, to piss the man off, was to flirt with death, or worse.

To receive a kick in the butt, a clubbing, or beating, was like a mere slap on the wrist. Compared to other things they could do.

Those poor souls who really pissed them off sometimes had a bad habit of just up and disappearing. One night as Delta lay on his bunk softly playing his harp, the door was suddenly thrown open, and the captain along with three of his henchmen came into the room.

They came directly to the bunk right next to him and unchained old Joe Harris. Then they just dragged him crying and pleading for mercy, away into the night.

Joe Harris was never seen again.

Joe was there for 'Trying to steal a can of sardines' and 'sassing' the store owner when he was caught. During that work day, he pissed the old captain off when he refused to commit an indecent act for him. That same night they came for old Joe.

Delta pretended to be asleep. Sure there wasn't one thing he could do. But you see, there are some things that will really trouble a man, and drive him almost to the point of insanity. He knew what was going to happen to poor old Joe, and he pretended not to see, for fear of his own hide. In that way, he joined the fraternity of the Three Monkeys: see nothing, hear nothing, and say nothing.

Poor Delta turned against himself.

Chapter 10

Chain Gang

They were working the main railroad north-south lines. Because of the war effort there was a lot of additional traffic on those lines, and they were in need of work to update them to the new standards.

The work had gone on for well over a month, and they were working an area that was pretty far away from any towns or ground level crossings. So whenever a train passed them you can bet it was high balling, or balling the jack.

Most of the traffic was freight trains carrying war materials both ways. When the engineers approached their work site, they always blew their whistles, and by that time everyone knew from the whistles which freight was coming, and where he was bound for. One thing for sure, those old boys were always on time.

Oh, I have to say it again. If only it was possible that you were there and able to hear old Jim sing and holler. Folks came from miles around just to hear him. The old captain would just close his eyes and rock back and forward in rhythm with Jim, and the fall of the hammers.

Oh, to hear those hammers ringing. There was something enchanting and heart lifting to hear those men singing, and following old Jim's lead man holler. And sometimes the long mournful cry of an approaching freight, with steam and smoke billowing in its

71

wake, plus the steady rhythm, and chug-chugging of the steam driving the many steel wheels against steel.

Even the creatures of the woods would stop to hear the songs of the chain gang.

But most of all, they came to hear Big Jim Yancy holler.

There was a main highway that ran alongside the railroad tracks, and where the distance between the highway and the tracks wasn't too far apart, folks would pull over, get out, and come near, just to hear those hammers ringing and Jim singing.

Shush, if you are real quiet, you can still hear those hammers ringing, and the men of the chain gang singing and following the lead of Big Jim Yancy.

> Take this old hammer and take it to the captain,
> Take this old hammer take it to the captain,
> Tell him I'm gwine, tell him I' gwine.

Listen to those hammers falling against steel, oh just listen to them ringing...!

'Water Boy', 'Go Down Hanna', and of course 'John Henry'. Oh, the sweet melody of those beautiful songs rang out and captured the minds and hearts of all those close enough to hear and feel.

I can still hear old Jim hollering, I can still hear those hammers ringing. Sweet Jesus, my heart is filled with those sad and glad memories, and mind-bending fears of those times. I have cold chills that come to caress and waken the dark sleeping memories tucked away in my heart. And I can't hold back the tears.

Oh, they laid some steel, even to this very day. There is no machine or automatic rail layer that can even come close to what that chain gang from Parchman Penitentiary could do. Most of the time they had the white gangs remove the dead rails and build the hump or bed. That's all they did.

The black gangs laid the ties, rails, and drove the steel. Listen to the hammers ringing, can't you hear those poor boys moaning. Listen to old Jim hollering:

Oh captain, huh! Oh captain, huh!
Watch my hammer fly, huh!
Watch my hammer fly, huh!

Oh captain, huh! Oh captain, huh!
Soon I'm gonna die, huh!

It's only my hammer sucking wind, lord, lord,
    Only my hammer sucking wind...

There was something about driving steel. Something that I don't have the words to express. There was a poetry of motion like the performance of one of the world's greatest ballets. Oh, to watch them work in perfect harmony. To watch their sweat-gleaming black bodies, straining under the pressure and mental anguish.

Swinging a heavy steel hammer and hitting the spike dead on, each time. To drive that spike into the wood crosstie or sleeper with unerring accuracy was indeed something to remember.

To hear them moaning, and answering old Jim's holler, to feel the pain and sorrow was to be a part of something that will live for ever.

From sun up to sun down,
Lord let those hammers ring.

'Blue bird when you get to Jackson go and knock on my baby's door' ... 'I got a cold black mare' ... 'Oh Lord how that horse can run' ... 'Just let me be your little dog baby till your big dog come' ... 'Well that mean old Frisco and that low down Santa Fe done took my baby away'. .. 'Rock me, Mama, rock me all night long' ... 'And night time is the right time to be with the one you love' ...

One evening three cars drove up close to the work site, and some white men got out and went over to where the captain was sitting on his special motor driven car with the big red umbrella. They interrupted his dozing and he was at first a little angry.

But after listening to what they had to say, he offered them a cup of iced water, and sent one of the screws to fetch Jim and Delta. He told them that the men were all the way from Hollywood,

California, and they wanted to listen to and record their chain gang working and singing. Plus they heard of Big Jim, and they wanted to record him.

They even brought a good guitar, a new harp, and neck harness.

Well, of course, Jim and Delta were happy to oblige. They recorded the gang working and singing. When that was done, they told Jim that his holler was the best they ever heard.

Jim and Delta did two numbers alone and two with some of the other gang members. When the recording crew packed to leave they gave the captain an envelope, which he promptly stuck into his pocket. They told Delta he could keep the guitar and harp, and he felt real bad cause all Jim got was a handshake.

That night after supper, Jim showed Delta the fifty-dollar bill the man sneaked to him when they shook hands.

The captain let Delta keep the guitar and harp, and that made his time after the episode of the Hollywood recording crew pass a little easier.

The first time Jessie came was a very sad time for both of them. After the tears, they had a few minutes to just enjoy being together. It was during that first visit by his mother that Delta found out why he only got three years for killing Charles.

It seemed that old Charles had rubbed the local law in Clarksdale the wrong way, and got away with it because of who his grandmother use to work for. In other words his grandmother had a very powerful protector in the Clarksdale white community.

So the local fuzz had it in for old Charles, and when Delta took him out he in fact did the man a favour. That's why he only drew three years.

Delta was allowed to play and sing 'as long as he didn't get out of line'. So he was able to pick up a lot of new material and meet a lot of new people who helped provide him the means to continue paying his dues.

The incident took place during the last six months of Delta's well over three years at Parchman. They were back on the main railway lines and had been there long enough for everyone to have full knowledge of the schedule for each freight train that went by them.

To the north of them was a rather large junction from which

some of the trains would go on into Alabama, Louisiana, and Arkansas, once they passed the junction. Most of the traffic went on straight north.

During the long time that Delta was there, he and Jim Yancy had become dear friends, and as Delta's time to change his clothes drew near, he thought painfully of the time that he would have to leave Big Jim, and he was very sad. He loved the man like a brother.

He didn't want to leave Jim, but he surely didn't want to stay.

That eventful day started off just like all the other days on the chain gang. For some unknown reason a few days before that day, the old captain had issued the order to put the ball and chain back on Big Jim. And old Jim just smiled.

Late that afternoon and shortly before quitting time, Jim led with 'Captain, oh Captain', two or three times, one right after the other. The men knew the old captain truly loved that song 'cause he knew when old Jim came up with the words that he had the captain in mind.

So the big boss man felt the song was in his honour. And the men felt that Big Jim was singing it over and over. Sort of like Jim was asking the captain to take the ball and chain off his leg.

It was all true up to a point. Yes, the old captain was really happy, you could see it on his face. Sometime later, Jim got permission to run off and do a 'two'. When he came back past Delta he shook Delta's hand and said:

'Young blood, you keep doing like you are doing and you are gonna get out of this hell hole OK. I want you to promise me that you won't ever come back here, and you'll keep on picking an' singing 'cause you are real good, and some day you will make a record. Maybe I'll come to see you someday when you've made it big.' He gave Delta a big knowing smile, slapped him on the back, and ran on back to his work place.

Something was out of order. He couldn't put his finger on it but something wasn't right. The way Jim shook his hand was like he was saying goodbye. And the smile on Jim's usually 'unsmiling' face...

They sang and worked on, I tell you, old Jim was singing his heart out, there was a feeling that just swelled the hearts of everyone there that afternoon. Why, even the guards were moving their bodies along with the rhythm of the singing and ringing hammers.

Great God almighty, they were laying track like they never laid track before. Old Jim's hammer was just a smoking, and the captain broke into a little jig and slapped his butt, he was so happy. Truth was, they were a full week ahead of his schedule. That fact was good for the captain and kept him in good with his boss.

Frankly, Delta was worried about Big Jim. Old Jim was acting kind of strange, and had a funny kind of light in his eyes, mostly when he looked at the money the Hollywood man gave him. He carried the money on his person all the time. Plus when the late afternoon freight bound for New York high balled past them, Big Jim would always pause to look longingly after it. Sort of like watching freedom pass him by...

Plus Delta noticed when that particular fast freight passed them, Big Jim would always stand dangerously close. That action on the part of his friend set him to thinking.

It surely wouldn't be the first time some poor broken and downhearted prisoner down on old Parchman Farm decided to jump in front of a fast freight, 'and let that Two-Nineteen pacify his mind', and take his life on to the Promised Land.

Maybe Big Jim Yancy was planning on killing himself.

Fact was, maybe a sudden death was far better then a slow humiliating death at the hands of the Man. It was all according to how you looked at it.

The engineer started blowing his whistle from way back. Oh, it was long and lonesome, the strange mournful sound tore at the hearts of every prisoner there. They could see and hear that great iron horse snorting and belching fire, smoke, and steam. Oh, that big black locomotive was charging down on them like the evening freight straight out of hell.

Everyone stopped work and stood clear in order to watch a sight that had stirred the hearts of men ever since the first steam locomotive moved on gleaming rails of steel.

The whole lot of them stood transfixed and watching that evening fast and long freight coming. That is, everyone except Big Jim Yancy.

76

Now old Jim was standing far too close to the tracks. The engineer just laid on the whistle. Like it was crying. Everyone else was safely out of the way. Except Big Jim, he just stood there smiling. Oh! Oh my dear God, NO! Delta whispered.

'Take this old hammer, take it to the captain,' Jim hollered as he threw his hammer back toward where the captain stood with his mouth hanging wide open.

The long blast on the whistle was like the engineer was saying, 'Boys, I'm booked out and bound to go, I just can't stop.' That old freight was really moving on.

That's when Big Jim made his move. He reached down and grabbed his old lady, his ball and chain in one hand, and then he jumped in front of that big black screaming and fast-moving monster. 'Oh my Lord, Big Jim is going to die,' someone yelled, and one big moan raised up from the men of the chain gang. While Big Jim raised his huge fist above his head and screamed defiance to the world . . .

At the last possible second, Jim jumped from in front of the speeding engine to the other side of the track, and out of the sight of his fellow inmates staring in horror at what they thought they saw.

Sometimes what you see is not what you see.

Old Jim stood safely on the opposite side of the long freight. Once on the blind side, he quickly moved to a certain position along the tracks and located the specific spot of his plans.

Then without so much of a thought about what could possibly happen to him, he waited for just the right time between the speeding wheels of a loaded box car and he threw his ball across to the inside, or between the two rails.

When the heavy ball landed on the rock bed it didn't roll, and Jim pulled the chain taut across the single rail and resting in the break between the ends of two rails, just like he spent days planning. He had left that break in the rail for the very same purpose which it was serving.

The wheel of the loaded box car rolled over the chain held in place by the gap in the rail and cut the chain as neatly as you please. There wasn't even a slight jerk on the portion of the chain that Jim was holding, or to the shackle around his leg. The heavy iron ball remained lying in the same place.

In one smooth motion Big Jim reached up and grabbed iron. He knew the freight wouldn't stop, it couldn't afford to stop. For, you see, coming right behind that old freight was the City of New Orleans which was one of the fastest passenger trains in the country.

The freight had to reach the junction and take its regular tracks before the City could pass it on by. That was the real big reason that old freight had to high ball on that particular section of track.

> And before I'll be a Slave
> I'll be buried in my Grave
> And go home to my father and be Free

Big Jim Yancy was FREE. Which proves that just because you are big you don't have to be stupid.

Jim Yancy rode that old freight train off into the sunset, and north to freedom.

> Gimmie a cool drink of water before I die,
> Lord, Lord, gimmie a cool drink of water before I die...

Just in case you are wondering.

Once the freight passed, and went on up the line, the men of the chain gang got enough courage to rush over to see what was left of Big Jim.

And there resting on the bed of rocks was his old lady, that big iron ball lying there was all that was left. There was no trace of Big Jim.

Then all at once they knew what happened to him. Fact was, Big Jim had escaped that awful existence down on old Parchman Farm. And he did it without a scratch, Jim was ALIVE. Most of all Jim was a free man.

They cheered, and cheered, some laughing, some crying, and some just standing there shaking their heads in awe at what Jim had accomplished.

He actually made it safely to Detroit, where he found work, and a new life. Jim worked in a plant making tanks for the boys overseas. He found a wonderful woman, married her and raised a family. He was a most respected MAN.

Big Jim Yancy was free at last...

Chapter 11

Mama

To be sure, it took a lot out of her, but Jessie came as often as she could. No matter what, she was there. After all she was his mother, and the fact that he was a prisoner in the state penitentiary didn't even matter. His mother stood by him.

'Even if the whole world should stand against you, if the angels of the Lord come to bear you away. Know one thing for sure, your mother will always stand beside, or in front of you, and offering her last for you to stay. Friends and lovers will come and go, but Mother will last as long as time itself. That fact I want you to know.'

Eight months and thirteen days after Big Jim broke free, Delta Sonny changed his clothes, and walked out the gates of Parchman Prison, his debt to society paid. He walked out a better man and truly not the same man he was when he walked in through that same portal.

Please note, I am most careful not to say that he was a 'free man'. 'Cause that would be very untrue, and a misuse of the word free. Oh, let it be known, for all eyes to see, for all ears to hear, and all minds to understand.

That once a man was forced to suffer the indignities and inhumane torture of being down on old Parchman Farm during those dark yesterdays, that man could never again be really a free man.

Sure he may have physically walked away from there and be

among the living. But don't let that fool you. For you see, that man was only 'half' away from the farm, the 'other half' was doomed to haunt the confines of old Parchman for as long as time shall endure.

Oh, can't you see the ghost of those poor souls breaking their backs on the chain gang? Can you hear old Jim Yancy hollering, 'Oh, captain, oh captain?' Can't you still hear those hammers ringing?

Look out! Watch it! There in the shadows and coming towards us is the ghost of the poor man who was strapped into the electric chair twice, and each of those times the chair refused to work and take his life. It was only after he begged God to let them kill him, that the chair worked, and his ghost joined those of all the poor other souls gone on before him.

Oh sweet Justice, where did you go?

The day they let old Delta out, Jessie was standing there waiting. She wore the happy smile of a dear mother, and the pretty dress he brought her before Mama Zula's prophecy sadly came to pass. You know, those shoes were still hurting her feet.

Percy stood always behind her, and patiently waited his turn, after she was through hugging her only son. Then Percy hugged him too. To be sure Delta felt the warm and firm embrace of the father that he never had. And the tears flowed like the mighty Mississippi.

When they drove away in the old battered pick up truck Jessie and Percy bought just for the sole purpose of coming to see him, Delta tried with all his might not to look back.

But he just couldn't help it, he had to look back.

> Take this old hammer,
> Take it to the captain.
> Tell him I'm gwine,
> If he ask you if I was running,
> Tell him I was flying.
> If he ask you was I laughing,
> Tell him I was crying,
> Tell him I was crying.

Yes, old Delta was crying as he stomped his foot, and slammed his hand against the truck's door in time, like the fall of the hammer against steel.

Oh, can't you hear those hammers ringing? One more time...

Chapter 12

Man

Many years ago, when I was a young boy, 'existing in the ghetto' ...
If you might happen to ask me to show you a Real Man, I would
have gladly and quickly pointed to, or given you the name of, one
of the guys down on the corner.

Oh, I thought they were all men, but you see, Old Sam Cooper
was my first choice of being the true essence of a Real Man.

Boy, Old Sam had already killed three men, shot two, and beat
the last one to death. Since he got out of prison he had six women
pregnant, three of them at the same time. Why old Sam had enough
illegitimate children for his own ball team.

He often said that he 'was the father of more kids than he could
count'.

Listen, Old Sam could cuss louder, drink more whisky, knock
anyone who was fool enough to go up against him, block clean off.
And say motherfucker right behind each and every word. Sam lived
on and off the street. He didn't believe in work.

Always said, 'Work isn't good for a man, if God wanted men to
work he would have provided a job for every man.' And since the
unemployment rate was high, that meant what he said was Gospel.

No sir! Sam said only suckers worked, and the Real Men 'took
what they wanted'. And I can tell you for sure he lived according to
his creed. 'Cause I often watched him on his daily 'pilgrimages'
throughout our neighbourhood, and sometimes went with him to

other places. When the working men of the neighbourhood went to work, Old Sam moved right on in to their sometimes still warm beds.

Women fought over him like he was a stick of peppermint candy. They even fought over who was going to get him next. Twice, and this is a matter of police records, women poured hot grits on their live-in men, 'cause the men got wind of what was going on, and wouldn't go to work so Sam could come in the house.

Boy, old Sam was one hell of a Man!

The women kept him clean as the Board of Health, and wearing two-hundred-dollar suits, Stacy Adams shoes, and a pocketful of bread.

In the summertime he often wore white slacks and dark coloured, sometimes special made, athletic, or muscle-type shirts. Of course the shirts and slacks were designed or cut to show off what he had to offer the women. You could see his big bulging muscles above and below, way before you could see him.

And he was always bragging that he was a Sixty-Minute Man or a Pipe-Layer Supreme. Once he got a woman in bed she was his for life, and that's a fact.

I'm not going to lie about it. Time was that I wanted to be just like old Sam Cooper. He was my hero, I looked up to him. I believed whatever he told me. If Sam said it was raining, I simply put on my raincoat.

Oh don't get me wrong, and think I was the only pig meat in the neighbourhood who looked up to him. Frankly, I think all of us youngsters, or pig meats as we were sometimes called, thought of Sam as our hero. He was our idea of a Real Man.

He didn't take no shit off no one.

Well, I said that to say this – thank God, or grand Providence, or whatever – that along my Road of Life, and while paying my dues, I had the honour and privilege of meeting some Real Men.

And you know what? They weren't at all like old Sam Cooper...

Now you take Delta Sonny for instance.

He did a lot of growing up while he wore the striped suit, and was married to that old ball, chain, and that ten-pound hammer. Way down there on old Parchman Farm.

Sure he didn't have big bulging muscles, hair on his chest, and probably wasn't a Sixty-Minute Man. And he wanted to work for whatever he got.

On the other hand, it goes without saying that he was truly sorry for his taking that which he wasn't empowered to give. A man's life.

So it was that Delta Sonny, the MAN, walked out the main gate of Parchman Penitentiary. From there he would return to Shady Grove, to Lightcap's, and to his mother's shot-gun shack.

He was alive. And that fact said a lot to his behalf.

He still had youth, health, and his dreams on his side. Which was one hell of a good hand, all he had to do was play it right. The old captain even let him have the guitar from the Hollywood crew. Jewel busted his old one, just out of pure meanness and hate. She swore that 'someday she would get even with him'.

So he had a new guitar, a new Fanny Mae.

On his first day home, he walked over to Shady Grove alone. Once he was there he stood and talked with the Spirits of the Dead. On his way back to Jessie's new place he stopped by the old one, just to look at it again.

The first Saturday night he was home, Jessie had some old friends over and they fried some catfish. Of course Delta and Percy provided the music, along with some of the other old Bluesmen from nearby.

Oh, they had a finger licking good time. Delta tried to play some of the new stuff he learned in Parchman. But the memories were too sad, he couldn't keep the tears out of his eyes and voice. Those years he spent there were like an open wound, and needed time to heal.

He played and sang of happier times, and did a lot of the stuff he did while on the move. Those were old standbys, and everyone there knew them. He did manage to do 'Big Boss Man' and some of the old Charlie Patton numbers.

Percy noticed right away that Delta had mellowed out, that his voice had taken on the hurt of the years spent walking behind a mule, picking cotton, and having to say 'yes sir' to assholes.

Around that time old King Cotton was in the process of falling from grace. There was talk of a new mechanical cotton picker, and chemistry, along with the march of time brought on by the war years, was producing a newer and cheaper way of making some fabrics.

The king was dying. Suffering from Acute Newitis, and old Father Time was tolling the bell. An entire system and way of life was about to fall, on its way out. Every Sunday at Shady Grove, the good folk noticed empty seats, and less voices raised to the glories of the good Lord. There was an ever increasing number of shacks standing vacant.

More and more of the good folk were stealing away to the Promised Land, north.

Delta helped Percy and Jessie around the house, in her garden and in the fields. Things were different, change was in the air, but there were those who were still trying to keep old Jim Crow on the throne.

While he was home the *Enola Gay* flew over Japan, dropped a bomb and shortly after that literally earth-shaking event, the war in the Pacific came to an end. That was around 14 August 1945.

And the changes brought on by the great war were sent reverberating throughout the land. Delta stayed home for a while and worked the cotton fields, until finally it got the best of him. The night and daymare that was the aftermath of his stay down on old Parchman Farm was so hard to shake. But after a while the long lonesome call of the whistle of a slow-moving freight caused the heavy load he was carrying to become manageable.

His original plan was to stay home till after Christmas. While he was in prison he often dreamed of sharing Christmas with his mother. But the sound of the whistle of a freight train flung a craving on him. The 'need' to reach up and grab iron. To smell the smoke from the engine, to hear the clickety-clack of the wheels. To ride the rails.

Oh, he and Percy played a few jooks and fish fries. But it wasn't like it was before, and during the war. Something was definitely missing. Most of the time the people didn't seem to be able to let go, to let it all hang out.

Those who came back on a visit from the Promised Land told too many stories of what it was like to stroll down Fifth Avenue. To shop at Sears or Goldblatt Brothers, to have access to good Sealed Whisky. The cover of blindness was lifted from our heads.

Whenever more than one person got together the conversation always seemed to wind up about 'going to Chicago'.

Well, one almost winter afternoon and during supper, he told Jessie that he was going to try his luck in the Windy City. 'Mama, I got to go!'

'Well, Son, to tell the truth, I'm surprised and most happy that you stayed as long as you did. It was good to have you close to me, so I could touch you from time to time.

'Now I know that killing that man is still riding you hard, and those long years on the chain gang and under the gun is still very much with you. But Son, don't forget what I always taught you: we all have our crosses to bear.

'Carrying your cross isn't what's different. But how you carry it is. That's life. So, Son, you go on to Chicago, and make your way up there. And it goes without saying 'cause you do know that I'll always be with you, no matter what.

'Now, Son, we come to the hard part, 'cause I want you to promise me that when you do go north, that you will go north in style. Boy, I don't want you to ride the rails.

'No, sir! I want you to go to Jackson and pay your way so you can ride the City of New Orleans, north.

'Please, Son. Do that for me, and don't you worry none about the money for your fare. I have more than enough left from the money you sent, and brought home to me. I still have almost all of it. I am going to give you enough so you can get yourself a decent place to live when you get there. Plus you will have enough to tide you over till you can get yourself a job.'

Chapter 13

Getting Started

For the first time in his life Delta Sonny rode on the train as a paying customer. Before that point in time, he said goodbye to his mother and Percy, then he took a Dog to Jackson, and purchased his ticket at the old I. C. station there on the corner of Capitol and Mill Streets.

You know, I just have to say this. It was kind of funny, when he grabbed iron and rode for 'free'. He could ride just about anywhere on the freight train he wanted to ride.

But, when he paid his fare and got a ticket, well, that's when the system dictated that he wait in the Coloured Waiting Room, and that he ride in the Coloured Passenger Car.

What was even funnier, the cooks in the dining car were all coloured, but he couldn't go to the dining car to eat what they cooked. 'Cause he was Coloured.

On the other hand, his shoe box lunch far outshined anything they served in the dining car. So there, now how about that for being smart?

When he got off the train at 12th Street Station, and went outside to take his look at the New World, he was stunned by its beauty. The beauty that was Chicago of that time and era. The air was already very cool, or at least it was cool to him.

He took his suitcase and went to stand outside and away from the bustling crowd. He stood in a position that allowed him the best view possible of the Loop, and downtown, or more correctly said, of Michigan Avenue.

He was impressed. To him the view was breathtaking and what he saw explained in some way why everyone who came back down home always had such exciting stories to tell.

He just stood there looking, or rubber necking, till most of the arrival crowd was away.

The taxi driver didn't ask him if that was his first time in Chicago. He knew that Delta was 'right out the cotton fields'. Said it was 'written all over him'.

Now Delta had a cousin living on the South Side at 44th and Indiana Ave. It was already arranged that she would put him up till he could find his own place.

So it was, that exactly eight days after he arrived he found a very nice one room kitchenette at 37th and South Park. His cousin's husband, Pete, worked in the stock yards, and due to his efforts, Delta went to work at Armor Packing Company. They started him in the hide cellar.

The first weekend after going to work, he took Fanny Mae and jumped Big Red on over to Maxwell Street.

Oh, I just got to say it here. During those wonderful years there was something extra special about Maxwell Street. Besides the fact that there was only one Maxwell Street just like that in the whole world. It was unique. Picturesque. And one of a kind to be sure.

Now some folk called it Jew Town, and some folk would say it was 12th Street, but actually it was just a little over 1300 South. But you could ride Big Red west on 12th Street and walk the short distance like most folk did.

There was always a big crowd of shoppers, bargain hunters, or people who just loved to barter. There was also a great number of folks who came for the sole purpose of being there.

One of the hallmarks of Maxwell Street was the food vendors. The outside stalls that sold the best sandwiches in all Chicago, in all the world for that matter.

I tell you the smell of the sausages, hamburgers, and hot dogs cooking, along with the wonderful aroma of great mounds of onions being cooked on the open grills would make you drool so much that the front of your clothes would look like you were caught in a sudden downpour, or heavy rain.

Please believe me, even if you just ate before coming to Maxwell Street, once you got there, the aroma of food would fling a craving on you, and you would just have to have one of something. Take my word for it.

One day I went over there and drooled so much my socks were wet.

Well, anyway, Delta got him one of those great long sausages on a bun that was almost too long to carry. Oh, he had so much stuff on it that to bite it hurt his jaws. With Fanny Mae slung across his back, he decided to walk around and look first.

Chapter 14

Maxwell Street

On his second pass down the street, he found two Bluesmen that he played with before. Once he stood so they could see and recognise him they asked if he would like to sit in with them.

Well, let's face it. That was exactly what old Delta was waiting for. And so began his Tour de Maxwell Street.

The little store, which sole a wide variety of everything including bundles of ten pairs of socks for a very low negotiable sum, was situated on the south side of Maxwell and some few doors down from the corner of Halsted Street, which was a very good location.

The owner of the store, which provided them space, electricity, toilet, and storage area, was a very nice little man. His name was Simeon Jacob Winestein, and he preferred to be addressed by his friends and associates simply as Simeon.

Now Simeon was a quiet little man with a great big heart. Plus the capacity to understand exactly what it was like to be a part of the wretched of the earth, and the outcasts of the world's society.

You see, Mr Winestein was also a fairly new addition to the growing population of Chicago. Incorrectly, there were those who thought Chicago was the Promised Land only to the black people. But during those times it was the Promised Land to people from all over the war-torn world. Especially from what once was Hitler's Fortress Europe.

There was a series of numbers cruelly tattooed into his skin.

Those numbers served to identify him, and his great suffering, and that he was a living part of the darkest episode in the annals of mankind, or perhaps humanity, or...

Simeon was unfortunate enough to come face to face with the Bitch of Buchenwald. He went to meet her along with his entire family, and when their meeting was over, only Simeon was alive to walk away. 'That place and those monsters robbed me of everything that was dear to me, and certainly much more than words can ever come close to explaining.' Simeon once told Delta those words.

When Delta and Simeon first met there was a true kinship that took place between them. That kinship was sparked by the great suffering and pain that was a part of both their lives. Oh, they didn't know it then, but that friendship would prove to be as solid as the Rock of Gibraltar.

Once they came to terms, Simeon provided Delta with an old folding chair and a nice soft pillow, 'cause 'Delta didn't have enough behind to soften the blow of long sitting'.

The arrangement went well, and Delta played Maxwell Street till the Chicago Hawk drove them inside. Which wasn't the same as being on the outside. There was something missing.

Still he made it through the winter. Oh boy, old Delta hadn't been so cold in all his life. He wore his long johns everyday, and two pairs of socks. Once while standing on the corner of 47th and Cottage, he was sure that was the coldest spot in Chicago.

But, it wasn't all for nothing, his time on Maxwell Street. One day he got to play for and with the great Muddy Waters. Some weeks after that time Muddy came to offer him the opportunity to do some back-up work with his group.

They played a lot of the bars and taverns both on the south and west side and Delta was happy 'cause that exposure gave him the chance to meet some of the real prime movers on the music scene in Chicago. Most of those prime movers were destined to become legends in their own time.

Such great names as Jimmy Rogers, Willie Dixon, Fred Below, the Myers Brothers, Jimmy Reed, and a whole lot more, which supported the fact that Chicago and Maxwell Street was the Mecca of the Blues.

The great Bluesmen came there from all over just to play Maxwell Street. Oh, I tell you that was a great time. Why you could jump Big Red and go there to hear such legends as John Lee Hooker, Lightning Hopkins, Sonny Boy Williamson, and Little Walter. Just to name only a few that come to mind.

There was always a crowd of people there to hear them play and sing. People who really appreciated the good old country Blues. Maxwell Street was the grand meeting place. The place where the Blues was offered in its purest forms, played outside in the opening and for the people, outside where God could hear every note, plain as day.

During those times it wasn't unusual to see some of the onlookers and listeners equipped with various forms of recording devices. Most of the time they would set their equipment up right near the artist, or aspiring artist.

Sadly, that was the time way before the true portable recorder as you know them to be today. But there were some people who would drag what they had over there to preserve for posterity the Blues history of Maxwell Street.

Many of the great Bluesmen were discovered while they played on that wonderful street of Blues and Dreams.

You know that was the time when many of the already established Bluesmen would go back to Maxwell Street in search of those new voices who were trying to be heard. And they helped them along the way, by giving them the opportunity that may have gone right on by. I like to think there was a true brotherhood in the Blues.

Some of the recording companies would send someone to keep his finger on the pulse of what was going on. That person's ear was attuned to what was new and good.

Unfortunately, to some people there was an unwarranted stigma attached to that good old down home form of music, that form of the Blues.

Sadly enough, I once heard an educated idiot refer to the country Blues as being Uncle Tom, backward, and wallowing in 'the misery of times best forgotten'. He was one of those fools who didn't want to accept the fact that the country Blues is just as great as any other form of music.

Perhaps some of the big recording companies also felt the same way. Perhaps there was a feeling that the country Blues only appealed to a small minority, and that minority was usually too poor to purchase a record, or was too busy getting up off the ground, too busy just trying to stay alive to buy a record.

Course there were those who mistakenly felt that the country Blues only served to remind them of something they would just as well forget. The down home music reminded them of picking cotton all day in the hot sun, of oppression in its foulest forms, of Jim Crow, and black bodies hanging from trees.

But thanks to those truly dedicated and pure Bluesmen, who gave their time, energy and for some, their very lives, to the proud heritage of the those good old down home country Blues. Yesterday and today...

May good health, good times, and the continuing sweet sounds of Little Walter's golden harp still echo on Maxwell Street, on those true Bluesmen of all times, and on those devotees of that golden area, for ever.

Listen! Oh, can you hear Jimmy Reed singing and playing, 'You don't have to go, big boss man, and honest I do.'

Delta knew he was fortunate enough to be a part of that history-making period in time. He was keenly aware of that long unbroken chain of devotees who were always there to hear them play and sing.

Truly 'the people, the fans, the devotees' were the main ingredients that made it all happen on Maxwell Street. And those legends of the Blues like Lightning, Jimmy, Muddy, Little Walter, Howlin'Wolf, and the chain of names goes on, and on.

All over there on Maxwell Street...

Chapter 15

The South Side

When the fresh coolness of autumn, that enchanting season of the year which is placed between summer and winter, to make the change over between hot and cold more easily made occurs. And the giant canvas of Nature's own is set to receive the beautiful colours from the magic palette of Mother Nature herself.

When the leaves are painted all red, gold and brown. When those leaves begin to fall, heavy from all those different colours of paint, we know that Mother Nature is doing herself proud.

That's the time my heart and mind always return to 41st Street. Where I see in memory's eye that which was. Always, shortly before the cold breath of the almighty hawk swoops down, and makes you know that winter is there.

Now old Delta sure enough added his voice to the voices of those complaining about how cold it was, but you know what? He really was enjoying that most beautiful time of the year in Chicago, and on the south side.

He wisely kept his job in the packing house, and many cold mornings while he waited for his El to work, he would be standing on the elevated platform all bundled up with so many clothes on that if he fell down, he would need help to get back up.

And that mean old hawk would still be kicking his cold butt. Just like he was wearing a bathing suit. One thing for sure, he could fully understand why Chicago was called the Windy City. That nick-name was most apropos.

Christmas was just around the corner, and people were slipping and sliding into the feeling of good will. There was a magic in the air, and he spent some time in solitude and appreciation of his new-found home in the Promised Land, and the true beauty that was really there. Oh, it was true there were no streets of gold, no free milk and honey.

But there was opportunity, certainly much more opportunity than there was in Mississippi. There was the opportunity to rise up from the ashes of slavery and old Jim Crow.

To be sure, there still were the undercover agents of the racist system that wanted to keep the black man a fourth-class citizen. But there surely was one hell of a lot better chance than down home.

His boss at Armor called him Mister Washington.

Mrs Carter, his landlady, was a real nice lady. A little bit eccentric, but nice. After his first week in her house, she always cooked enough food for him. And when he came in late she would even get up and warm it for him. She refused any additional money for feeding him, saying that she 'had to cook anyway, and it was just as cheap to feed two as one.'

She even did his laundry, and wrote letters home to Jessie for him. You might say that Mrs Carter was his Chicago Mother.

Well anyway, Delta felt right at home in his new surroundings, and Mrs Carter was so nice and helped him so much. He often played on the West Side, but he felt out of place over there. Now when he was back on the South Side he always felt much better.

From 31st Street North and South to Riverdale, Chicago Heights, and Gary, Indiana, he played house parties, wakes, and weddings. Oh, there were so many of the good folks from down home in those areas. Some of them were incognito, but around two a.m., and when the Blues was just flowing like water, the chitterlings was about all gone, and someone broke out the White Lightning, they dropped their mask, and got on down.

Man, it seemed that most of the folks from the delta were by that time in Chicago, and more than half of them were on the South

Side. From around 31st Street and extending South to 35th and 43rd Streets, and from State Street East to Cottage Grove, and in some cases all the way over to the Lake, were a great number of down-home folks. That area could have very well been called 'The Little Delta'.

Why not? Chicago already had its Little Italy, Little Ireland, Little Poland, and China Town. Why not a Little Delta? In that area bordered by those streets that I named was a very true and real feeling of the Mississippi Delta and down home.

Sure there were a lot of folk from Alabama, Georgia, Louisiana, and even Texas. But, the folk out of the Mississippi Delta far outnumbered anywhere else.

That time was the beginning of the House Party Period. Most of the new arrivals were working and earning more money than they ever saw in their lives. Perhaps it wasn't that they were earning so much money, but the fact that where they came from if they saw twenty dollars all at once, that was a lot of money.

So it was that immediately following pay day they wanted to celebrate their good fortune. That was the time to come together and have a good time, to have a party, to jook.

Oh you see, the term 'party' was used instead of 'jook', 'cause the word party had the proper sound, it was more up-north, more city, and dignified.

Why, everyone knew that 'jook' was pure country and lacked class.

Sadly enough that was the time when a lot of people who did more for the state of Mississippi and the grand old South than anyone else ever did, were forced to leave the only home they knew, just to be able to exist with some dignity.

Most of them were ashamed of their delta heritage, their being from Mississippi. During those times there was a very popular saying. It went something like this:

'If you must be from somewhere, be from anywhere, as long as that where, is not from Mississippi.'

You know, sometimes I think that little abstract saying often served a dual purpose for a lot of people. I think in some cases that flamboyant saying served to hide some of the true hurt that was present in the hearts and minds of a people who were subjugated to the point that they were forced to abandon the only home they knew. To take flight and leave all their few earthly belongings to whoever may want them, to steal away riding on a dream they couldn't even see.

Walk in their shoes for a while, then tell me how you feel.

Home is home whether it's a cardboard box, a nice apartment, or a shot-gun shack, no matter how you look at it, it's still home. There were many of the good folk who were trying in vain to hide the awful hurt that was eating them alive. So I guess they just partied down to hide what they really felt.

That's where the Bluesmen came in; you see the country Blues was that little bit of home that came to Chicago with them. The pure sounds of home put to music.

I'm a poor boy long, long, ways from home...

Music was an essential part of our lives down home. There were those good old gospel songs that we sang in church, at funerals, and when we felt a need to talk to God. To ask him why. Then there was a need to just throw your head back and sing, to holler the Blues.

Lord, Lord, I ain't going down that lonesome road all by Myself. Must I holler or must I shake em on Down. It must be a Bed Bug, you know a Chinch don't bite that Hard.

The Blues was the life blood that flowed through our veins, and was as such an essential part of being black. It was and is the music of Africa, our Motherland. And brought to America in the hearts of our poor people forced into the cruelty of slavery and down in the cotton fields of the Mississippi delta.

The Bluesmen were then the heart, the pump that maintained the pressure to make the blood of the Blues flow through our veins, and in that way they kept us alive, way up there in the Promised Land.

98

Oh, if you could have attended only one of the many house parties that went on every Saturday night in the Little Delta.

> Don't tell me where you came from,
> Just tell me where you are going.
>
> Big boss man, can't you hear me when I call.
>
> Mama cooked a chicken, thought it was a duck,
> Put it on the table with its legs sticking up.

And while the good folk were shaking 'em on down the fish was frying, the chitlings, pigs' feet and ears were almost ready. The crackling bread was in the oven.

Sure, most of the good folk had moved up to sealed or store-bought whisky. But I tell you truly there still were some purest who preferred to make their own. Grandpa often said, 'There ain't no whisky in all the world as sweet as good corn whisky, specially when you make it yourself.'

My Grandpa had a class A still right there in his basement. Once the batch was right and Grandpa was down in the basement, it was best for your health to leave him there till he wanted to come upstairs.

To tell the truth, there were a lot of stills in our neighbourhood, leastwise some of the folk that I knew had their own still. Some of them were in the basements, some in the attics, and there were a few in the bathrooms.

Matter of fact, there were two stills in the apartment building closest to the police precinct station.

The area bordered by 31st Street, Cottage Grove, 43rd Street, and west to State Street was the best party/jook area, if you were looking for some good old down-home getting on down. The music you heard most in that area was the Delta Blues. And most of the time those Blues were played by some of the greatest Bluesmen of all times. You could always hear the voices of Leadbelly, Jimmy Reed, Muddy Waters, Lightnin' Hopkins.

And many, many more. Later there were the sounds of the Enchanted Harp of Little Walter, and Sonny Boy Williamson.

There was that solid beat of John Lee Hooker. The Howl of Howlin' Wolf, and many, many more.

Course, the farther South you went the more the good folk tried to cross over, to be what they surely would never be. Most assuredly not in that lifetime.

One thing for sure, the parties around 31st Street were unequalled, cause they were just being themselves. The food was pure Mississippi Delta, and after you greased down there was only a good time to be had by all.

Now old Delta played some of those house parties, wakes, marriages and funerals. There were rent parties, car payment parties, bail bond parties, pink slip parties and I got to get out of town parties.

Why, he even played at some of the local bars and taverns. Some of the Bluesmen in Chicago were already regularly playing at some bar, tavern, or club. Because such an arrangement provided them with a steady paycheck.

Plus, such an arrangement also allowed for them to have a known place from which they could be seen and heard.

The South Side was alive with the music that made the people happy. Country, or Delta Blues, Chicago Blues, jazz and all kinds of other contemporary music, not to forget Gospel and that new stuff called Be Bop.

That was also the time of the music and voices of such legends as Ella Fitzgerald doing 'Robin's Nest'. Of Lady Day singing 'Good morning, Heartache' and 'Willow Weep for Me'.

There was also the music of Charlie Parker (Yardbird), and Lester Young (Prez). Not to fail to mention Johnny Hodges, Earl Bostic and Paul Quinichette, just to name only a few of the greats.

Music completely surrounded you. Wherever you were, you could hear 'Moody's mood for Love', 'Take the A Train', 'Stomping at the Savoy' or 'Lullaby of Birdland'. All that backed up by the voices of Billy Eckstein, Arthur Prysock and the great Nat King Cole.

Oh I just have to say it: 'The South Side was beautiful.'

They were all there for you to hear, for you to see, for you to dance to their music. Every Saturday night the great ball rooms were jumping. Or, you could walk into a quiet place and hear Al Hibbler, go to the Chicago Theatre and thrill to the golden voices of Sarah or Peggy Lee. Or, join a group on the corner and Du Wah in the still of the night.

The beat of the great heart of the South Side was music, and that's where the greats of music always came together, and the walls of ignorance and prejudice began to crumble.

And it was all right there on the South Side of Chicago.

Chapter 16

Done Got Over

The deal was too good to turn down. Besides, he had waited a long time for just such an opportunity. They signed the agreement only four days before Christmas.

He had promised himself that he would be home with Jessie and Percy for that special day. But necessity dictated that he change his plans and break that promise.

The club wasn't very large, or one of the more famous clubs on the South Side. However, it did provide him with a steady income based on his music and how he met the public. His end of the take was a bit less than what his pay cheque was from Armor and Company. But his fringe benefits, and advancement to his career as a Bluesman were most substantial.

Unfortunately, the arrangement necessitated his having to let his job in the stock yards go. So when he quit Armor he made it so that he could go back to work there if things didn't work out. He told them that sickness down home was his cause for leaving.

Now, you must remember that while he was there he worked like a Georgia mule, always on time, and never once gave those appointed over him a hard time. Fact was that old Delta was a model worker, and that fact stood him in good. They said that he could always come back there to work.

Never burn your bridges behind you. 'Cause you never know when you may have to cross those same bridges again.

By that time he had saved a few dollars, some from his job and some from his picking an' singing. Oh, he never forgot to send some home to Jessie on a regular basis. That went without saying.

The first full night on his own gig was a good one. No, the place wasn't 'packed'. But those who were there seemed to really enjoy what he had to offer. When he looked out to them he saw his home folk from the delta, and he knew what they wanted.

By that time, and while on the road paying his dues, he learned to watch the faces of those he was playing for, and from their expressions and their eyes, he could tell what they wanted and most of all if he was giving it to them.

It was all right there in their faces.

The proof of the pudding was the following nights, when he and the manager saw the crowd grow and grow. Right on up to standing room only.

Delta Sonny was out there on his own, and making it. He thought of an old Gospel song he often use to hear his Grandma sing:

> I'm so glad I done got over
> I'm so glad, I done got over at last.

Christmas in Chicago was just like in the movies. Everywhere the fresh snow covered everything like a never-ending beautiful white blanket. The air was cold and clean as it lifted on high the sounds of the Christmas song being elevated to new heights by the marvellous voice of Nat King Cole. While there was the joyful Christmas tunes for the children, and Miss Mahalia Jackson sang, 'Oh Holy Night' for all the world to hear.

Everywhere he went he was surrounded by the beautiful sounds of Christmas. And everyone he met greeted him with 'Merry Christmas'. He met people singing in the street. And you know what? Most of those happy people were singing for themselves, or perhaps the person or persons who was with them.

47th Street was all lit up, nice and pretty, as was 63rd and some other main streets. Of course State Street downtown in the Loop was on top of the hill, so to speak. But those streets on the South

Side were also very beautiful, and Santa Claus at South Center department store was black, an African American.

That one fact alone made Christmas in Chicago, and more specifically, Christmas on the South Side of Chicago a momentous occasion for Delta Sonny.

Mrs Carter cooked a wonderful down home Christmas dinner. It included, but wasn't limited to, chicken and dressing, Delta nut cake with fresh black walnuts all over the place, hot rolls, candy icing cake and lots of tater pies.

Now Delta asked Mrs Carter if he could invite Mr Winestein for Christmas dinner and she said, 'Yes.' When he asked Simeon to come, at first he was hesitant, saying that he 'didn't want to impose'. But Delta talked to him some more, and Simeon said, 'Yes'.

Oh it's quite true that Mr Winestein may have celebrated Christmas differently and at a different time, but he came to Delta and Mrs Carter's home and they had a most wonderful time together.

Jew and Gentiles came together under one roof to honour the Christ child and to shout joy to the world, the Lord has come.

Oh, let me let you in on a secret. When he first went to Mrs Carter for the room, she said that she was a Native Chicagoan. But all that proper stuff had slipped, and when she cooked Christmas dinner, it was all over. The cat was out the bag.

And old Delta knew for certain that Mrs Wilma Carter was from Mississippi, to bring it right on down front, she was from the delta.

You know why he knew? 'Cause no one, but no one, can cook a delta fruit cake, or nut cake, specially with whisky soaked into it, and with black walnuts, like they cook them in the delta. Except someone who grew up with that kind of delta cooking.

Let's face it, the candy icing, and tater pies wrapped it all up. You see there is something special about a Mississippi delta sweet bread and sweet potato pies that absolutely can not be duplicated, nowhere, no time, no how, period...

When he told her how good the food was, and that it all had that delta flavour and goodness, she just smiled and said, 'Thanks.'

It was what she didn't say that came across the loudest. Wilma was delta, she just came to Chicago before him, and they both knew it.

Simeon brought a bottle of homemade wine, and peppermint Schnapps. They celebrated well on into the night. Oh, they didn't forget. They went to the Greater Harvest Baptist Church for services.

'Jesus the Light of the World, and Jesus my Rock.'

Also there was an added bonus to that special Christmas. Mr Winestein and Mrs Carter hit it off real well, and by the time he was ready to go home, Wilma and Simeon agreed to see each other again.

The New Year brought Delta even more acclaim. But it was still too early for that elusive contract. There were a whole lot of other good Bluesmen out there in Chicago and the record companies could afford to be real choosy.

Sure, he recorded as back-up for some of the best known names in the City, and for some of the top labels.

But, up to that point in time, he never had his own contract.

Shortly after Easter Sunday he formed his own permanent group. Someone suggested they call themselves 'The Mule Skinners', but those were the times that no one wanted to be country, or from the country.

So they finally decided on the name. 'The Bluesmen'.

Now old Delta surely did receive some lucrative offers from some other clubs, and taverns from as far north as Milwaukee. But those offers were mostly hit and run.

So he chose to stay right where he was, with the people who gave him his original break. And like all the other Bluesmen, he often went back to Maxwell Street to play, and see who was new.

During his stay at the club Al Benson became a regular, along with some other Chicago notables of that time. Al even gave him some plugs on the air. Sometimes he would go to the West Side and play with Muddy, and sometimes Muddy would come and sit in with him.

Things were going well for Delta in the Windy City, and on the South Side. He then had an account at the First National, and was driving a brand new Dynaflow.

105

There was a nice newly renovated flat on 51st Street, which he could very well afford to move into. However, Mrs Carter's was home to him and he chose to stay there.

The great migration away from the cruel hell of the police state, and the oppression of old Jim Crow, was by that time in full swing. There was a headlong rush to the relative freedom of the north.

It's true, that freedom was mostly a dream, a figment of the imagination, but anything was better than the hell we were existing in. And at that point in time, the nation and its industry, which of course included the job market, was winding down from its war time posture.

When it was called upon, America's industrial giant rose up, and stood head and shoulders above all the other nations of the war-torn world. The great War was over and then it was time for the magnificent giant to go back to sleep, perhaps never to wake again.

Added to that situation were the thousands of victorious veterans returning home and hoping to fill the rapidly dwindling vacant job slots. Oh, to be sure, the influx of people literally rushing into the city of Chicago was, to say the least, staggering.

And that grand rush would at a later date bring a beautiful city to its knees. Oh, if only the city fathers were clairvoyant, if only they had the vision to see farther on up the road.

Perhaps then, the Once Upon a Time Story would by this time have the traditional happy ending: 'And they lived happily ever after...'

But, too soon the party was over. The jobs disappeared, but the people didn't. And the devil found work for their idle hands. Crime ran rampant, the gangs grew into a many-headed snake, the zip gun into a 38 Special, all along with a complete disregard for the law. And brother rose up against sister, and son against mother and father.

Great God almighty, what a time.

Even Delta couldn't help but see the differences, since the time he got off the train at 12th Street Station. He saw it in the faces of the people he sang for on a nightly basis. The smiles wasn't the same. The laughter was often soaked in tears.

Gradually there were more fights in the club, and more people

106

drinking too much in an attempt to hide their frustrations and their resentment at the hand old Faith dealt them.

There were too many poor and jobless people in too little space. There were too many idle minds and hands, overcome by their growing frustrations, and resentment at the hand old faith dealt them.

For some the Promised Land was turning into a night and daymare: too much, too soon, too little, too late.

The gap between those who had, and those who had not, grew ever wider.

Of course Delta drove down home to see his mother as often as possible. Jessie and Percy were doing well. There were some favourable changes in the situation, and they even had electricity in their old shack.

Delta tried to talk them into coming back to Chicago with him every time he was home. They always said, 'No.' He knew the only way he would get them to move would be to hog tie them, and physically put them in the car.

However, after him seeing the changes on the face of Chicago, he abstained from asking them, and decided to leave well enough alone. To leave them where they were.

Her name was Willie Mae Thomas, and he met her while he was playing a special party in the Gardens. And since that time he moved part way into her apartment with her.

I say 'part way', 'cause he refused to give up his place with Mrs Carter, or Mom as he was by that time calling her. Willie Mae and Delta got along just fine, he even took her down home to meet Jessie and Percy. They liked her very much.

Now it was mainly through Willie Mae that he made some of the rounds of Chicago's night life outside that of Little Delta. They went to the Blue Note, the Chicago theatre, to see Sarah and Billy.

Be Bop was crashing the scene, and the Battle of the Bands was the place to see and hear such greats as James Moody, Thelonius Monk, Illinois Jacquet, and Sonny Stitt. An excursion down town, then, to the Argon, Savoy, Pershing and Trion Ballrooms would produce the wonderful sounds of the last of the Big Bands.

And you could hear the voices of Ella Fitzgerald, Peggy Lee, Sarah Vaughan, Tony Bennett and Al Hibbler.

Delta's repertoire had grown to enormous proportions, with some of the new stuff reflecting the Chicago sounds of the Blues. Of course some of the works were there only to make the almighty buck.

He found the old traditionals or standbys to be the best foundation, and the people seemed to prefer them. The old favourites were still that little bit of down home that meant so much to so many.

Sure, there were some new names on the block, but most of them still did the old Blues. The Chicago style was often called for, but not as much as the oldies.

When he did 'Devil in the Woodshed', 'Poor Boy' or 'John Henry', he could see the expressions of those who missed the real delta. And when he did 'Blue Bird', 'Highway 49', and 'Haunting', smoke would get in a lot of eyes. Including his.

To be sure, the crowd's reaction was always electrifying.

Well, I'm broke and I'm hungry, raggedy and I'm dirty too
But if I clean up, pretty Mama, can I stay all night with you.

Chapter 17

The Tolling of the Bells

All things considered, life for Delta was going well, the weight of killing Charles was lessened to a 'you can live with it' level. The horrible nightmares caused by his tenure of existing over three years at Parchman Penitentiary were also a little less.

At least he only woke up screaming once or twice a week. And he even went back to church.

Still, though his name did appear on some of the record jackets of the more famous Bluesmen of that time, his name was there only as back-up or sideman, playing his guitar, harp, or vocals. His dream of a big fat recording contract for a top record label, and him as solo artist, still eluded him. It was still only a dream.

Maybe his taking that which he didn't have the power to give was dogging him. Maybe Jewel had a spell put on him. 'Oh, if only Mama Zula was still alive,' he often thought to himself. Whenever he had those thoughts of her it always seemed to him that he could hear her in his mind and heart saying to him, 'Boy, you got to really believe, and when you do I will be there for you. Remember that morning in the box car.'

Once when she was alive, she told him, 'Boy, the strongest muscle in your body is your brain and to believe is to be strong and survive. The old ways are not always superstitious nonsense, but rather a way of life that is as old as mankind.'

Irene goodnight, Irene goodnight,
goodnight Irene, goodnight Irene,
I'll see you in my dream.

I ask your mother for you, she told
me that you was too young.
I wish the Lord that I never seen
your face, I'm sorry that you was born.

Delta had the honour of meeting the Legend while he was in New
Orleans and staying with Mama Le Beaux. That was the time that
he was on the road.

Now old Leadbelly knew Buddy Washington from the old days,
and he was very happy to meet young Delta. They sat down and
played, and played. When they played together there was always a
crowd of people come to enjoy their Blues. Mama Le Beaux's house
was always full of the faithful.

Now it was during those times that Delta and Leadbelly went
over to play in Shreveport, Alexandria and Baton Rouge. Then they
came on back to Mama Le Beaux's where they got some sleep before
playing a big house party over in Algeria.

They played 'Big Fat Woman', 'Looky, looky yonder', 'Black
Betty', 'Poor Howard', 'Green Corn' and 'Bring Me a Little Water
Silvy'.

They also liked to do together the classics like 'Grasshoppers in
my Pillow', 'Back Water Blues', and of course 'Take This Hammer'.

Sometimes when they did 'Take This Hammer', they would
travel back through the tunnels of time. Back to those dark days
when they both wore the striped suits of the dammed and had the
shackles on. 'Cause they were both steel-driving men ...

Needless to say they became fast and evermore friends. They truly
enjoyed playing together, the master and the student. Before long
Leadbelly left, going back up to Mooringsport, East Dallas, and
then on to New York City.

Delta knew for sure that he was privileged to sit in the giant
shadow of a real Legend of his time. The one and only Huddie
Leadbetter, who was already known by everyone as Leadbelly.

Now you know old Delta never forgot those wonderful times of his playing with Leadbelly, and he closely followed his idol's career as the bright star shot across the heavens.

He was so happy for Leadbelly when he heard of him going to such lofty places as Harvard, and some of the other distinguished institutions of higher learning.

Why old Leadbelly even went out to the coast and Hollywood, California, playing his 12-string guitar and doing such great things as 'Good Night Irene', 'Take This Hammer', and 'Ella Speed'.

I can tell you, Delta really loved Leadbelly the man, the Bluesman and the Legend. Those are some of the reasons why old Delta cried like a little baby child when the word came that Leadbelly was dead.

Sweet Jesus, Delta hadn't cried so hard since Buddy died. It was like he couldn't hold on no longer. Well, it took some time 'fore he could get hold of himself to think that old Leadbelly was making the journey that he surely had to make some day, that the long journey was still his to take.

Yeah, old Leadbelly got on up and left Bellevue Hospital, took his guitar and like the po' boy that he surely was, he went on down that lonesome road all by himself, and down to the River. Just like we all got to do.

Lord, I'm a poor boy and a long, long ways from home,
And I ain't gonna be treated this a way.

Oh, let me tell you. Huddie Leadbetter aka Leadbelly was the essence of the term 'Legend'. The man and his music was and is as much a part of America, Americana, or any other way to say it, as any other famous, or widely known persons that America produced. And that goes for everyone, black or white, past or present, living or dead.

He carried the torch of the Blues and held that torch so high that the light shone all over the world.

He was an extraordinary person, a Bluesman supreme, an African American, and his wonderful gift to the American people constituting the total sum of us all, that gift shall never pass away.

There is a whole lot of heart and soul in the lifetime story of Huddie Leadbetter, the poor boy, the man. A story that should be

111

told to America now, and preserved for all the coming generations. For is it not true that the story of Huddie Leadbetter is a story of America? Think about it.

And to those African Americans who might think they have only the dark days of slavery to fill the history books of their being in America, tell them that their cup runneth over with the pride and passion of such men as Leadbelly, Lightnin' Hopkins, Muddy Waters, Son House, Robert Johnson, Blind Lemon Jefferson, and the names and accomplishments are truly endless. God Almighty, lift every voice and sing...

Shout it from the rooftops, and tell your children the fact that the Blues is the foundation for well over fifty per cent of all America's contemporary music.

Tell them that only in America could such a story as that of Leadbelly come true. And not to forget the one man of true foresight who had the presence of mind and the perseverance of heart supported by his great love of the Blues.

For him to seek out such great Bluesmen as Leadbelly and many, many more in his never-ending quest to preserve the enchanted heritage of the Blues.

That man presented the voice and soul of the Blues to the America that the wall of stupidity stood too high for the Bluesmen to reach over. That man took Leadbelly with him on his song-gathering expeditions up the length and breadth of America and made it possible for those who might never have the opportunity, to hear the soul of the Blues.

To hear the voice, the 12-string guitar, and the Blues as played by Huddie Leadbetter the Legend. He is gone, but his voice is still with us.

Toll dem bells, oh toll dem bells...

Delta arranged for a special night of them good old down home country Blues to be played in Honour of Leadbelly. Oh, oh that night was a night to remember. Many of the Chicago Bluesmen came to pay their respects to the memory of the great man.

The Little Queen of Clubs (the club where Delta worked) was

packed to standing room only, some folk even stood outside on the street, just to be near.

And Chicago's family of Bluesmen came to be united in song. Muddy, John Lee, Sonny Boy, Lightnin', Bukka, Howling Wolf, Lonnie, and many, many more.

Oh, the stars shone so bright that you could see for miles and miles. Little Delta was all lit up like a Christmas tree. The Blues rolled like thunder, and at the same time floated on the gentle breeze like a beautiful red, black and green feather.

The guitars, harps, drums and voices all blended in to bring down home on up to the Little Delta, in tribute. The Blues filled the night air like never before.

> Oh there's six white horses in bound,
> They's going to take me to that burying ground.
>
> Oh ring dem bells, and ring dem loud
> Looky, looky yonder see him there
> Standing on that cloud.
>
> If I had the gov'nor where the gov'nor got me
> Before daylight I'd set the gov'nor free.
>
> I beg you gov'nor upon my soul
> If you won't gimme a pardon
> Won't you gimme a parole...

Chapter 18

Vengeance

After the sadness of losing a dear friend was eased by the passage of old time, Delta and Willie Mae were married in a quiet little ceremony. And in record time she gave him the good news that she was pregnant.

Of course they were both very happy, and began the happy task of getting ready for their new baby. Now she was a Registered Nurse at Provident Hospital, and planned to work right up to her time.

The occurrences I'm going to tell you about, happened while she was working the night shift.

The correct Chicago time was two-fifteen in the morning, and he had only minutes before laid down and was almost asleep, when the clear voice said to him:

'Boy, you git out that bed and run down to the hospital, your wife and baby are in certain danger.'

Delta sat straight up in bed, his mouth suddenly gone dry. He was wide awake and shaking like hell. 'Cause what he saw caused his blood to run cold.

She was standing near the foot of his bed, and dressed in the exact same clothing she wore when they buried her.

He suddenly had to pee real bad.

Delta rubbed his eyes, even though it wasn't at all necessary. He saw what he saw. 'Now, boy, don't you sit there like a knot on a log, like you never saw me before. I done come a long way just to warn you. Now it's up to you what to do.'

In an instant she was gone.

No! Mama Zula didn't look like some bug-eyed Hollywood version of a zombie. Hell no, she looked exactly the way she looked when he last saw her and she was considered alive.

'It's only a dream,' he told himself, 'I've been working too hard, and I know Willie Mae is OK. Otherwise someone from the hospital would call.'

Generally, the night shift during the middle of the week was pretty quiet, a Sunday School picnic, compared to the weekends.

Still, he decided to call the hospital, specially when in his mind the memory of that early morning standing in the box car in the New Orleans railroad yards came flashing back, and properly jerked his chain.

He even tasted the flavour of the Black Cat's bone and salt as he charged into the bathroom before he drowned.

Then, suddenly it was all very clear, and that clearness galvanised him to action. He cursed himself for a fool again, because he lost faith in the old ways. He failed to believe. Willie Mae *was* in danger.

On his way out the door and still putting on his clothes, he worried that he may be too late, and all because of his doubting the undoubtable.

If they passed out degrees for stupidity, he would hold a Masters.

Willie Mae came to the phone in answer to an urgent female voice who begged her to 'Please step outside in the rear of the hospital near the back ramp'. Because a dear old friend of hers was sorely in need of her help. She was asked to come alone, and her friend would explain everything.

She did as requested. That wasn't the first time one of her friends had come to her for medical assistance and a promise never to tell. She rushed out the rear doors and after a minute, or two, she saw a woman bending over and clutching her stomach like she was in great pain.

Willie Mae couldn't see the woman's face, as the apparently wounded person staggered towards where she was standing. Clearly the woman was indeed in great pain. But because she was still in the darkest portion of the alley near the trash cans, Willie Mae could only assume the woman was who she thought her to be.

'Dorothy! What's wrong, are you hurt or cut?' She ran down the ramp to meet the huddled figure of her dear friend as Dorothy sank to her knees, and at the same time a loud pitiful moan escaped her lips.

Shortly before reaching where Dorothy was kneeling and crying, two men jumped from the shadows and grabbed Willie Mae. One man clamped his dirty hand over her mouth and stopped her first scream. He held one of her arms in a vice-like grip, while the other man took her other arm and they dragged her back into the darkest part of the alleyway.

They threw her to the hard pavement and began ripping her clothing off her body. Their intent was perfectly clear.

She fought in desperation, her fear giving her added strength, as she bit the dirty hand that was covering her mouth. Even his blood tasted of cheap wine. She screamed and fought like hell, but to no avail.

'Please, please, I'm five months pregnant ... Please don't kill my little baby!' She pleaded and begged, as the man she bit struck her.

'Dorothy, please help me!'

When the first of the two men mounted her, and in the midst of her pain, shame, and struggling, she caught a quick but plain glimpse of the woman who had lured her to be violated. That woman wasn't her friend Dorothy. That was the first time she ever saw that bitch grinning down at her, and urging the men to 'Tear her ass apart!'

One thing for sure, if she survived through the ordeal, she would never forget that grinning face.

They were rushing Willie Mae to the OR when Delta broke through the doors. 'Oh my God, Wil, what in the world happened?' he screamed.

Through it all she didn't lose faith in herself, or lose consciousness, she fought the bastards all the way. Matter-o-fact, her kicking and screaming her head off was what saved her. Because of the early morning quietness, and two of the other nurses seeing her go out the back, as they heard her screaming she was saved.

116

Added to that, while the first man was trying to get it in, her grasping hand found a nice chunk of cement from the nearby construction site. The solid piece fit quite nicely in her hand, as she proceeded to whip the piss out of the guy on top of her.

The first blow closed his left eye. The second shattered his jaw bone and knocked out some teeth, while at the same time busting both his slobbering lips. A tooth and his wine blood fell into her face.

The seriously wounded less-than-a-man bellowed in pain. He screamed for help, as he blew blood, bits of broken teeth, and slobber all over the place.

His sexual desire went, limp as a wet noodle.

Before the other guy could stay her hand with the hunk of cement, she inflicted even more damage on her assailant by hitting him square in his big nose. Blood shot out and almost blinded her.

Course, by that time she was mad as hell, and even though she was almost blind by the guy's blood, she had no trouble finding her target. Her accuracy was undeniably true, and on the bad guy's head and face with each telling blow.

She struck him on his Adam's apple, and that was all she wrote.

By that time the guy on top of her wished he wasn't there. The pain and lumps on his head drove away all his sexual desires. He was no longer trying to gain penetration but fighting like hell to gain separation.

The tide turned, and he was struggling for his very life. His screams of pain added to her screams of rage, and together they woke the entire neighbourhood.

The totally beaten bum rolled off her, as he tossed his cookie. And her final act of defiance was to rupture the other man by kicking him directly in his balls.

Now, his screams really did rattle the garbage cans and bounce off the walls all the way down to 51st Street. He fell to the pavement, rolled into a foetal position and screamed bloody murder, while almost choking on the bile that flooded his mouth, and nose.

His hands clutched what used to be.

Help from the hospital was rushing out the back doors and towards them. The woman was screaming curses at her inept duo of

117

rapists while she and the thoroughly beaten first man dragged the neutered second hood towards the closest end of the alley.

Everyone heard a car start, then drive away with tyres screaming and rubber burning.

When Willie Mae saw Delta she really started to cry, not that she was in so much pain. No sir, she was crying because she was so damn mad about what those two bastards tried to do to her. And that damn woman was definitely in charge and she fell for her shit.

She was also very angry that her co-workers had the opportunity to see her naked, and all covered with blood and broken teeth. At the thought of the broken teeth she just had to laugh out loud.

'Cause she had the immense satisfaction of knowing that she whipped the bastard who was trying to ride her to a fare thee well. She whipped him like he was a stepchild.

Oh sure, she had a fat lip, a black eye, and some other bruises sustained mostly by the fight she put up, and the fact that she had to do it all while on her back.

Who said that you can't get results while lying around?

The sheet covering her nakedness was soaked in blood, and the doctors and nurses had no way of knowing if that blood was hers or her assailant's. Still they paused long enough for Delta to comfort his wife and brush away her tears, before they wheeled her into the emergency room.

Sometime later and after the police arrived to question her about what happened, she was all cleaned up, and was given a clean bill of health. Except for mostly minor bruises, the loss of a perfectly good uniform, and the embarrassment of being seen in her birthday suit.

She was all right. The doctors felt that no harm had come to her unborn baby, and that the pregnancy would proceed quite normally. Everyone was relieved.

When she could, she told Delta and the police exactly what happened. Then when she and he were alone she went over it again, to include the best description she could give of the woman. Unfortunately, the police admitted there were no real clues to the crime, except for the broken teeth. Her description of her attackers could fit about ninety per cent of the vagrants, winos and hoods on the South Side, or in the entire City for that matter.

Their chance of bringing them to justice was so slim, you couldn't even see it.

However, after all that was said and done, there remained some intriguing unanswered questions, like:

A. Why was Willie Mae singled out for the attack? The fact that was exactly what happened was as plain as the nose on your face.

B. Who were the two men? It seemed they were hired help. So who was paying for the job, and why?

C. Who was the woman, and why was she after Willie Mae?

Those questions screamed for answers, and quite frankly were in a position to hurt the good relations between Delta and Willie Mae.

Chapter 19

The Bad Penny

It's very true that sometimes female fans of people, or more correctly said, female fans of men who live in the limelight, often go to the extremes regarding their feelings for their Idol.

So it was that the first thought was the attack on Willie Mae had been carried out by one of Delta's over zealous female fans.

However, to attack his pregnant wife the way she did was a little bit much. And one couldn't but help to think: was the woman a crazy fan, or was she just plain old crazy, or, now this is the big one, was she an old flame?

Now Willie Mae, or Wil as he lovingly called her, asked those same questions, and when she got to the last part, about the old flame, there was a long pause in her speech, and all the while she looked him directly in the eye.

After a long pause on his part, and being very careful not to break eye contact with his wife, he answered her this way:

'Wil, you are not the first or only woman I've been with since I came to Chicago. But, since I met you, I have never been with another woman. And before I met you I've told you what was going on.

'Now Wil, I tell you truly, according to your description of the woman who led the attack against you, the description doesn't even come close to anyone I ever knew before you.

'Sweetheart, you are going to have to take my word on that.'

She did, and they were able to move on from there.

The afternoon of the next day and before going to the club, Delta sat in his kitchen having a sandwich and coffee, while his mind was reviewing the events of the attack on Wil. There were many possibilities of strange crazy women. But his gut feeling kept telling him there was a dead cat on the line. That the woman was after him, and not after his wife.

Sure, there was always the possibility of some woman who may have a grudge, or a crush on him. But his mind and heart ruled that all out. No, the woman was definitely after him, and she wanted to hurt him so bad that she was willing to destroy his unborn child, and maybe his wife in the process.

Who could hate him so much?

His Delta Survival Senses told him that he was up against an old enemy. A bad penny that was coming back to haunt him.

In his mind he went back over the description of the woman in the alley, his mind drawing a mental picture of the one woman his senses kept telling him had masterminded the attack.

But his mental picture of that woman was painted the way she looked when he last saw her. And that was before he did time in Parchman. Then while he was putting his dishes away, something told him to age the person in his picture and don't forget to add a few pounds.

He did just that to his mental picture and when he saw the transformation he knew he was right. 'Cause his hands shook so violently the cup he was holding crashed to the floor. The revelation of what he saw in his memory's eye rattled him to the core.

The bad penny was none other than his first love. The added age and pounds did the trick. He knew who the promoter of the alley attack was.

God knows she had the motive, was fully capable, and was right there on the West Side. He knew she was there, but he thought that after all those years she had buried her hate and forgot, or forgave.

But no! Now she was stalking him, she went after Willie Mae, because he took Charles away from her. He could still feel her strong hands holding him so her Charles could take his life. He heard again

121

her foul mouth screaming curses at him, and saw her hate-filled eyes. Remembered her saying, 'You Mother—er, I'll get you someday.'

The bad penny was Jewel, she was back, and seeking revenge.

That night at the club he actually did only two numbers, and let his band carry him. His mind and heart just wasn't there. He was trying to figure what Jewel's next move would be. And what he could do to stop her.

You see, Delta hadn't told Willie Mae all about how he wound up in prison. No man wants people to know that he was played for a fool, and most of all for them to know that the fool in him came right on down front.

Now that mistake or fool was coming to bring him down.

His best course of action was to get ahead of her, to find her before she could strike again. He would confess all to his wife after it was all over, but then, the time wasn't right.

Early the next morning he drove over to the West Side, and decided to drive around a bit hoping that he might spot her. Oh, I might add that old Delta did a wise thing when he borrowed his friend's car to drive over there with. He figured that if she knew so much about Wil, she would surely know what car he drove.

Well, he drove around for over two hours, and nothing. After a few more streets, objective reasoning kicked in, due to the fact that Jewel had called Wil at work and called her by name, plus she knew the name of Wil's dearest girlfriend.

He didn't have to look for Jewel. She had already found him. And had watched him for a long time for her to plan the attack in the alley so well.

The best thing for him to do was to watch his own home and tracks. She would come to him, she would trip up somewhere, and he would be there to catch her. It was an old delta coon hunters' trick, to double back on your own trail and wait.

Thus began the game of cat and mouse. Only it was no game; old Delta was serious as a heart attack. And he was the cat.

Well now, it took over two weeks for her to break cover. Wil was back to work and doing OK. He was carrying on as usual doing the same things and going the same route to and from the club. However, he was watching his back, and doubling back on his trail and waiting.

Sure enough, it all paid off.

Early one Thursday morning, and when Wil left for work, Delta sneaked out the house from the rear, and rushed down the alley to the corner so he could follow her all the way to work.

Now you see, he counted on the possibility that Jewel was watching his house and had their daily routine down pat. She would know that normally once Willie Mae left the house, he would go back to bed and sleep a few more hours.

His old enemy would also know when Wil had the day or night shifts. And most of all he figured that since they had remained quiet about the rape attempt, Jewel would think that he and Wil just wanted to forget that whole thing.

He counted on that line of thinking on Jewel's part to make her complacent, to make her think she got away with her crime. Thinking that way she would become sloppy and that's when he would jump on her with both feet.

Well anyway, about five minutes after Wil turned the corner, he spotted a woman who definitely was following her. He worked in close to be sure, and saw without a doubt the woman following his wife was indeed Jewel.

His first love, his sad past, was back to haunt him. Vengeance was her name and Delta was her game.

He kept her and Wil in sight till Wil entered Provident Hospital and work. Jewel even went and stood by the door, as if she was trying to decide whether to go in or not. Then she suddenly turned, and went back to her car.

The broad was certainly all brass. During the entire time she was following Wil she never looked back on her own trail. She was dead certain she had the situation well in hand.

Delta moved in close enough to see her plain as day. And close enough to bring her down, just in case she was planning on going for Wil herself. She sat there with the motor running while she seemed to be in deep thought.

That's when he took a good look at the car, and suddenly a lot of things fell into place. The car she was driving was an unmarked police car. He knew where to look for the serial number, which was #J-523. The car had a police radio, and a non-stationary red light.

Jewel was a cop, or she had access to an official police car.

Regardless of whether she was a cop, or had access to the car, with that revelation came the answer to a lot of questions, and he began to understand how she managed to know so much about him and his wife. She had the resources of the Chicago Police Department to back her play.

Quickly he followed her to the precinct where she parked the car and went in. After that he drove slowly back home, his mind running full out with all the possibilities.

He knew where his enemy was to be found. She had run true to form, the West Side was her stomping ground, and like a creature of habit she only ventured to the South Side in her quest for vengeance. He figured that once she passed State Street she was out of her element. And that was to her disadvantage.

The Little Delta was his element, and to his advantage.

Wisely, he decided not to tell Wil what he knew. A few days later he talked Willie Mae into staying home till the baby was due, and he also arranged for Mrs Carter to be with her.

Now he told Mama Carter what was going down, so she would know what to look out for. But still they didn't tell Wil.

He set out to gain as much knowledge as possible about his enemy. He followed her both night and day, and all the while he kept book.

Yes. She was a cop.

And yes, she was using her position as an officer of the law to hurt him and his family.

No! He didn't go to the police with what he had. Such a move would prove fruitless, and tip his hand that he was on to her. You see, another advantage that was definitely in his favour was she didn't know he was dogging her.

He decided his best course of action was to watch, and wait for her next move.

Willie Mae and their new daughter were home from the hospital

124

only the second week when Jewel struck again, and believe me, that strike was a hard act to follow.

*　*　*

It was near the end of the second week and Mama Carter had a doctor's appointment so Wil was home alone with the baby. She had only minutes past fed her, made her comfortable, and the little baby was sleeping soundly till her next feeding, or cleaning, whichever came first.

The house was very quiet, and Wil was in the kitchen fixing something special for Delta, who had gone shopping for her. Once she had a few minutes, she decided to sit quietly and enjoy a hot cup of coffee, while waiting for him to return.

When after a few minutes, and like new mothers all over the world, she went to the baby's room to check on her, Wil slowly opened the door and went quietly over to the crib to peek in, her world dropped out from under her.

Her beautiful little baby was gone!

But, the crib wasn't empty. There lying where she last saw her baby sleeping peacefully was the rotting, maggot-infested and stinking carcass of a huge grey rat.

Willie Mae grabbed her head and screamed, and she screamed, and she screamed. Her mind, heart, and body overloaded. Because she didn't have the luxury of fainting. She came within a hair's breath of going around the bend.

Fortunately, Delta was very near with his arms full of groceries when he heard her screaming, which urged him to run into the house and find a scene that was right out of his worst nightmare, and taxed even his mind.

'My Baby, My Baby, Oh my dear God, somebody took my Baby!!!' Wil screamed as he burst into the room. She fell into his arms, exhausted, and her voice was cracking and almost gone from the strain.

A hurried but thorough look around the room confirmed his worst fears. Their baby was gone. While thinking quickly, and knowing that his wife was teetering on the edge, Delta had to use great force to drag her from the room, and close the door.

All the while she was screaming, and screaming.

All the while he was dying and dying.

How could one person do such a thing to another person?

A neighbour called the police, and much to his surprise the police were on the scene within minutes. They were very professional, and seemed as much revolted by the presence of the rotting rat and its position in the baby's bed as anyone.

Detective Sims was called, and even he was there within a short time. He vowed to catch the culprit or culprits. By that time there was an ambulance and doctor also on the scene.

Willie Mae was given a strong sedative, but the sedative wasn't helping at all. Twice they tried to get her to lie down, but she refused. The police were questioning the neighbours and, on the instructions of Detective Sims, they were told to search the house as well.

Finally and close to total exhaustion, plus maybe the sedative was finally beginning to take hold, Wil agreed to go to the hospital. 'Cause I just can't fight it any more.' She said that just before everyone clearly heard the distinct tiny voice of a baby crying!

'My baby! that's my baby crying,' Wil shouted as she broke loose from those who were trying to help her to lie down so she could be carried out to the waiting ambulance. The restraining hands were as nothing, as she rushed toward the sounds of the baby crying.

The little baby was tucked safely away over behind some boxes in a closed closet which had already been checked, and the person checking the closet had absentmindedly left the door slightly ajar. If the door had been left closed, well perhaps it would have been another story. But as it was, they could hear the tiny baby crying for its mother.

Once the mother and baby were most tearfully reunited, and the dead rat was taken away by the police, even the bed or crib and bedding were removed to be destroyed.

Wil and the baby were transported to Provident Hospital where she was given a private room, and Mama Carter moved in with her, resolving never to leave her alone, 'not even to go pee'.

Delta told the police that 'he had no idea who would do such a thing'.

Delta lied.

Because there was no hard evidence to tie Jewel to either crime. How she got into the house he had no idea. However, the old man next door said he positively saw a woman enter and leave the house.

But he thought nothing of it 'since he saw the same woman there before, on other occasions'. But he couldn't give a good description of her 'cause his eyes were bad.

All in all, Delta still didn't have anything to go to the cops with, specially when he would be trying to bring down a cop.

No. He would have to do the job himself.

Later that same day he sat in the hospital room watching his wife breastfeed their little daughter. He knew for sure. That a change had to come. They just couldn't go on that way. Something had to give.

'Cause sooner or later someone had to die. There would be a sad song and a slow walk. The thought of killing her was rapidly overtaking his sense of decency and restraint. To kill again wasn't something that he welcomed. But she was pushing it, and the code of the Delta dictated that she die.

Later he sat alone in his kitchen busily weighing the odds.

One. He could take his family and run. Maybe go North to New York, or South back to the Delta and Belzoni, Jackson, or maybe on down to New Orleans.

The big problem with that option was that he had spent well over three years of his life, down on old Parchman Farm, just-a-paying for what he did. And let's not forget that old Charles was trying his level best to put that switchblade into Delta. All that, while Jewel was holding him for the deadly kiss of Charles's knife.

And to run away just didn't set with him. Besides he had no guarantee that she wouldn't just follow him and make his life a living hell. Hell no, the code of the Delta was very clear, that he blow her away.

There was no way he was going to run. No way in hell.

Two. He could go to her and ask her forgiveness, apologise, and offer her some money. Try to buy her off. Of course the problem with that option was that she could always change her mind at a later date, and come back on him.

Three. He could simply bring her down, kill her and be done with it. Hire a wino or, better than that, go over to the North Side in Little Italy and put out a contract on her. That way he would not have to dirty his hands. But, oh dear God, how it would dirty his heart.

Let's face it. Option three was by far the best. 'Kill your enemy today so you won't have to face him tomorrow.' He could just lay in wait for her, jump out, blow her away and be done with it. The law would think someone that she leaned on in the past finally got to her.

That she got it in the line of duty, she would go out a hero, and no one would bother to look in the closet.

The only problem with that option was that he didn't want to kill no more. His conscience was already overloaded.

The telephone rang, and he rushed to answer it. Maybe it was Wil. The person on the other end of the line chose to remain silent, but didn't hang up. And sure as hell, he knew who his caller was.

She finally had to savour her victory. To return to the scene of the crime. She needed to know first hand that she had hurt him. A mistake on her part.

'Jewel, I know it's you, and I know that you are responsible for the attack in the alley behind the hospital. That it was you, and only you who took my baby. That was a cowardly thing to do, even for you ...' He had to hold himself in check, it would not be too wise to push her.

'Jewel, can't we talk? I'm really sorry about ...'
She slammed the phone down. He waited, thinking she would call back. But nothing.

After waiting more than two hours, he gave it up and decided to take a hot bath, maybe it would help clear his head. So that he could decide on the best of the three options for him to take.

However, once he walked into the bedroom, the luxury of taking time to decide was snatched from his grasp, and the options were narrowed considerably.

Jewel had struck again!

Some of Willie Mae's underwear was scattered about the floor, and each pair was ripped to shreds. Seemingly with a knife. Also the wedding photo of him and Wil was mutilated.

The baby's room didn't fare any better.

The third option sprang to his mind and heart as he went to get his 38. It was past the time to bring her down. 'That bitch was in this house within the last few hours. No more games. It's time to kill her,' he said aloud.

He ran out the door to his car and drove straight to the West Side, to the twenty-six hundred block of Warren Boulevard. Once in the vestibule he simply pushed a few buttons, and waited. Someone buzzed the main doors, and he was in.

While almost running up the stairs to where he already knew her apartment was, the soft gentle voice of his Mother Jessie, came clear as a bell to his mind.

'Son. Don't do it. If you do, you will be playing right into her hands. This is a situation that you can't win, not this way. Boy, you got a good wife and new baby girl just a waiting for you. THINK!'

He stopped dead still. His heart pounding so loud he thought everyone in the building could hear it. The pain of killing Charles, and the memories of Parchman flooded his heart as he did the right thing and stopped to think.

Then he slowly walked up to the door of Jewel's apartment. Trying very hard to flush the anger out his mind so he could objectively deal with his enemy.

He knocked gently on her door, after having made the decision not to blow her away but rather to try and talk to her. The voice of his mother came right at the most critical moment, and prevented him from making a most grievous error. One that he would have regretted for the rest of his miserable life.

Jewel answered his knocking on her door. And it was all right there in her eyes. She was expecting him. Delta knew for sure if he had rushed in to kill her the deal would have gone down just like the wise voice of his mother said.

Thank the dear Lord for good mothers.

She stood looking at him for a long time. And he couldn't help but see that she was holding her service revolver, which looked like a police special, 38 calibre, in her right hand and down to her side. If he had kept his pistol in his hand she could have shot him in self defence, but because she didn't really know if he was armed, she was waiting for his next move.

Old Delta knew for certain that his life was held in the balance. If he went for his iron, she would surely take his life. He saw that in her eyes along with all the insane hate.

He had to walk easy.

'Come on in,' she said, as she moved back to maintain a safe distance between them. And not bothering to hide the fact that she had her gun in her hand.

'Long time no see,' she said, her eyes holding him fixed like a hungry vulture.

'Yeah, it's been a long time,' he said.

'Why have you come here to my house, you dirty bastard you? Is it 'cause you want to screw a real woman. 'Cause you want to beg my forgiveness?'

'No! I didn't come here to screw you. Jewel, I know it was you who hired those two guys to rape my wife in the alley behind the hospital. And you did that to my baby, plus you were in my house only hours ago. How do you get in?'

'I got a key just like you have, matter of fact I got keys even to your car. Yes, god damn it, I did all those things, and that ain't the half of it. There are some other things that I did that you don't know about. Yet.' She was fighting to control her anger.

'OK, so I'm guilty as shit. What you going to do about it? Beat my ass? Kill me? Or fuck me to death? Go on, admit it, I'm the best piece you ever had. You poor dumb country bastard, where is your little greasy mojo bag now?

'I was just playing with you. When I met you I needed a man to fill the gap till I got back to Charles. Charles was my real man, the only man I ever really loved, and you, you stinking son of a bitch. You had to go and kill him. He was the only man who could satisfy me.

'Well, I'm going to pay you back in spades for what you did to Charles an' me. And at my own time I'm going to kill that bitch you are living with.'

By that time she was almost screaming. The hand she held the gun with was jerking violently, like she was close to pulling on him.

'And, if I don't change my mind, I'll kill that little brat of yours so you can see her just like the rat I left you,' she added.

There was madness in her dull brown eyes, and that madness showed through the hard glare of pure hate.

Jewel was way around the bend, and way past reasoning. She was a mad dog in need of killing. There was no other way.

Now I'm telling you truly. He wanted to go ahead and pull on her. To take his chances on her getting him first. Figuring that he would get her before he was done for.

His hand was twitching, he wanted to pull his pistol. Only pure reasoning held his hand back. Delta smiled at her, and turned to leave the apartment.

She was like greased lightening, as she moved to stand between him and the door. And old Delta came face to face with the cold one eye of death in the form of the barrel of her 38. She had him dead to right. Her hand shook, and he could see her finger tighten on the trigger. Old death was very near.

But she made the mistake of stepping even closer to him, and he took the only option left open to him. He slapped the gun away from his face. She fired.

The sound of her firing that first round was drowned out by the passing siren of an emergency vehicle. The 38 slug buried itself in the wall.

He wrenched the gun from her hand, almost taking her fingers with it. She yelped in pain, anger, and frustration. 'You son of a bitch,' she muttered through clinched teeth.

He forced her down on one knee, while fighting the urge to break her damn neck.

'You best go ahead and kill me now, 'cause if you don't, I'm going to wipe your ass with a buzz saw,' she growled at him, her voice dripping with menace.

Delta placed the barrel of her own pistol in her mouth. Her eyes grew to the size of silver dollars, and her hole was so tight it almost disappeared.

He slowly dragged back the hammer.

She swallowed, and wet her panties.

He smiled. No, he grinned. It was time to end the charade...

Then he thought of Big Jim Yancy, of Parchman, of his wife, child, and of his mother.

No, there just had to be a better way. To kill her was to kill himself, and all his dreams of the future. How would he explain it all to Wil? Already there was the distinct possibility that she wouldn't understand what was happening to her. Because he had lied to her about his knowing that Jewel was behind the attacks on her and the baby.

Already the truth was too small to cover the lie.

To kill her would be his one-way ticket to Joliet, and the end of Delta Sonny.

He removed the dripping barrel of the 38 from her mouth. She collapsed on the floor. Then he carefully removed the cartridges from the cylinder, walked over and threw the pistol as far back into the apartment as he could. He knew that she may very well have another gun close at hand and, as she was again standing watching him, when he passed her, he laid one on her, brought it up from the floor and caught her square on the jaw. She went down, and it would be some time before she regained her senses.

Delta checked the hall both ways, put the night latch on the door and closed it, then he quietly slipped away. There would be another day . . .

Chapter 20

Another Day

All the way home the shakes persisted; his hands were actually sweating on the steering wheel. He was so close to blowing her head off. And paying the price of which she wasn't hardly worth.

One thing for sure, she was surely coming after him. The proverbial cat was out of the bag for sure. My how she changed, that real good-looking girl he met at Piney Woods, and couldn't get enough of her loving, the woman that he actually killed a man for because he caught that man screwing her. His first love, his first mistake.

In their last encounter he took her pistol away from her, and went upside her head. In the essence of the word he scorned her, and that was a definite no-no.

And you know what they say about a woman scorned. It was going to be hell to pay, and it was all going to come out of his pocket.

Now, old Delta knew he had only a short time span to do his thing. He didn't figure she would come after him right away. Basically, Jewel was a coward. All people like that are. She thought he would be on full alert, and expecting her to come running to him in a fit of rage. So she would wait and hit him when he wasn't looking.

He counted on her thinking that way. 'Cause if she did, it would provide him the valuable time to get ready. Oh, I'm not saying that he wasn't ready, if she did act the fool that she was, and did the unexpected.

Which would be for her to try and do him before he did her.

While sitting at his kitchen table he checked his shotgun and .38. It was while he was doing that when the clear-minded thought came to him.

Yes. There was most certainly another way.

'Oh, boy, it surely took you a long time to come to the right conclusion,' the gentle voice of Mama Zula came across the table to him.

She sat right across the table from him. A great big smile brightened her wise old lovely face. Anyone who might have been able to see her would have accepted her presence as possibly his grandmother sitting at the table with him.

When in fact Mama Zula was a ghost, a haint, a spook, a spirit. A whatever you might want to call her.

She pushed the pistol and shotgun away with a quick look of distaste on her face, as she said, 'Now we don't need these things. You give me those bullets that you took from that She Satan's gun. You know she had to touch them to load her pistol, and I need something that she touched.'

Delta took the cartridges from his pocket, truth was he forgot he had them. He slid the five live cartridges and one empty across the table top to her waiting hand. She reached out and covered the mound of cartridges with both hands.

'I shall keep her away from your house and family till you can do what you have to do. But I warn you, this spell is limited by the strength of your belief in the Old Ways.' Then, with a mischievous twinkle in her eyes, she was gone.

Delta put his weapons securely away, went to bed, and got the first good night's sleep he had in months.

The new day brought the clearest mind and heart he had since the attack in the alley. First he would bring his wife and baby back home. Mama Carter was already with them and would stay with them till he got back.

To get away from the club wasn't a problem. However, to come up with an excuse as to why he had to go down home and at that

134

particular time would be a problem for him to explain to Willie Mae.

Another lie was required. Or, he could just tell her the truth about what was really going on, and about his involvement with Jewel. He decided not to tell her the truth.

Instead he told her that word came that his mother was very sick, and calling for him. He had to go home to see her as soon as possible. Of course Wil believed him, and told him to go home right away. That she would be OK.

So the day after Wil, the baby, and Mama Carter came home and was settled in, he told her the police were watching the house, and that he was going to the club to arrange for his absence. Oh, he did stop briefly at the club, but mostly to pick up one small item which would be his key to what he had planned.

From there he drove directly to the West Side, and Jewel's precinct station. Just to be on the safe side he parked over a block away and walked to the precinct. Just in case he might accidentally run into her. At that stage of the game he wasn't leaving anything to old chance.

Before he entered the building he knew his first line of deception was for him to act like he owned the place, like he was some big wig from 12th Street, or downtown, and there on official business. He cradled his key (which was nothing more than a normal clipboard with some old inventory forms from the club's storeroom) in his arm, and held his pencil poised like he was itching to use it.

The ruse worked. Not one person stopped him, or asked his purpose. Everyone seemed to be doing their best to avoid him. The clipboard would do it every time.

After looking around to orient himself, he just followed the signs to the locker rooms; the women's section was walled off from the male section. He marched right into the locker rooms with purpose, and found her locker about half way down the aisle.

The cheap combination lock was child's play, a pushover, and he had it open just like that. When he had the door quietly open, he was sure he would find all that he required.

Jewel definitely wasn't a neat person. The inside of her locker looked like someone stirred it up with a stick. And he stood back, just in case something big and bad jumped out.

What he came to get was right there before him.

A. Her comb and brush from which he took some of her hair left clinging to each one. Boy, she was losing a lot of her hair.
B. A bar of soap in a plastic dish, from which he found three curly pubic hairs which were clinging to the soap.
C. A pair of white wool socks draped over some well-scuffed and stinking tennis shoes. He took the socks one at a time, turned them inside out and shook the dead skin and even a small piece of her toe nail into the third waiting white envelope, which he sealed immediately just like he did the first two.

Everything was replaced just like he found them, the lock was snapped shut. And he walked arrogantly, right out the front door.

It's a fact that people will rarely stop or question a man with a clipboard. Specially when he has a pencil poised to write it all down.

The items he collected were from Jewel's own body and were her essence. Or as we might say today, those items were her DNA.

For those of you who may not know it, the items Delta collected are often those asked for by a sorcerer, a hoodoo person, or a witch, if one were to go to him or her seeking a spell, or maybe a love potion.

Anyway, once he was back home, he packed a small overnight bag. The three envelopes were carried on his person, so as not to take even the slightest chance of losing them.

After saying goodbye to his family, he went to 12th Street Station and on down to New Orleans. The trip down was uneventful, except when he knew that he was nearest to Jessie and home. He considered getting off at Jackson and paying someone to take him to Belzoni so he could tell his mother what was going on, but he didn't have the time to spare.

He couldn't call her because his mother didn't have a phone, and the nearest phone to her was in the Lightcap's general store down in the settlement.

No. He had to chance it that Wil would take his word about Jessie being sick, and that she wouldn't make any inquiries on her own.

When he arrived in New Orleans, he went directly to Mama Le Beaux's house. She knew he was coming, and when he asked how she knew, she smiled coyly and said:

'A little bird that sat at your kitchen with you a few nights ago told me.'

First he took a bath and washed with the special homemade soap she gave him for that very same purpose, and to cleanse his body without.

After his bath he ate a bowl of fresh collard greens and rice, with hot peppers to cleanse his body within. He was forbidden to use a fork to eat with, but rather she told him to eat with his fingers, delta style.

When he was finished eating, she told him to go into his room, close the door, and draw the shades, so that he could sit in the darkness. He was told to meditate on what it was that he wanted to do.

In that way, he would become one with his honoured ancestors and their gods. Also that he would become united with the single purpose of his visit. In that way he would cleanse his soul.

Mama Le Beaux came to get him when the time was right. And she had already made the necessary arrangements to get him to the House of the Seventh Sister.

Before crossing the water to go over to Algiers, he had to first step over a fine line of salt, and a freshly cut green branch at the same time. The branch had to be cut from a young tree in an old cemetery.

When the preparation for the JuJu ritual was completed, he took only the three envelopes with him and he crossed over into Algiers, where he was taken directly to a certain house which sat at a certain location. And the man who took him was dressed all in black.

That house was the House of the Seventh Sister.

The House of Sister Anjei.

A sorceress.

A witch.

A hoodoo woman.

A Mama Loa, and sacred high priestess.

'Step over the fresh grave seven times, and drink the still warm blood of a fighting cock. Raise your right hand up to the midnight sky, and call to the great father three times: *Igazi, Invanga, Insimu, Itulu...*'

Chapter 21

Spell

'Mosquitoes all round my bed, keep me way from my whisky an beer.'

The small room was completely void of all furniture and the normal things that you would expect to find in a room. Situated at what appeared to be the exact centre of the floor and room was a homemade circular enclosure, which consisted of a wood fence which stood only about six inches high, and the pickets were nailed close together like the staves of a barrel. They were placed that way to contain the earth which filled the entire circle, and that earth was packed hard through constant use. The ring or circle appeared to be about eight feet across, and the earth was flat.

The perfectly round enclosure was filled with earth from a cemetery, or burial ground, and that earth was taken when the moon went from old to young, the last day was Friday, and the date was the 13th. The time was midnight, and the taker of the earth was of the living dead.

Placed at the centre of the hard-packed earth was a round blood-red rug with ancient African juju symbols woven into the red, using the black hair taken from a full-grown goat. There were other sacred symbols and drawings along the border of the rug and on the smooth and polished wood floor.

Those symbols were devoted to the gods of voodoo as that sacred religion is practised as Santeria in Cuba, Obeah in Jamaica, and Orisha in Brazil.

Sitting at the centre of the rug was a clear glass bowl which was about three quarters full of clear water. And near the bowl, sitting in an earthen saucer, was a single lit candle. The candle was positioned so the light from its flickering flame shone through the bowl and water. There was also the distinct pleasant odour of incense and oil.

Oh, I almost forgot, there was one thing on the windowless walls. On the wall facing the doorway where Delta stood, looking into the room, there was hanging a mummified leg and foot, which once belonged to a proud fighting cock.

The sacred fetish was hanging from the blade of a sugar-cane knife, which was piercing a large fancy white-laced handkerchief and imbedded in the wall. The handkerchief was affixed to the wall so as to form a white background, thereby making it easier to see the dark, almost black, sacred object.

Delta was allowed to stand in the doorway and look into the sacred room before he was told to enter; that was a part of the ceremony. Another part of the ceremony or ritual took place before he reached that point.

The man in black brought him to the front door, knocked on the door in a prescribed manner, and left him standing there alone, and without a single word of goodbye.

After a brief pause, the door was opened by a smiling little old white-haired man of undetermined age, who politely asked him to 'Please, come on in.' Soon as the door was closed behind him, the little old man began the initial cleansing ritual.

When that was over, he instructed Delta to remove his shoes and socks, and to hold the three white envelopes in his hands so that the bottom envelope rested in the palm of his left hand, and his right palm rested against the top envelope.

Then and only then was the door to the special room opened and Delta told to 'Stand here and wait a few minutes.' The little man stood silently directly behind him.

After the few minutes, the little man told him to 'Go over to the rug and sit down facing the chicken foot'. Delta did as he was instructed. The man closed the door, and there was the distinct sound of a bar being put in place. He was locked in the room alone.

It seemed he was sitting there with his legs crossed and hurting like hell for an eternity, before the flame of the candle suddenly went out. Delta held his breath, and the envelopes, like it was his last hold onto reality. Something that was slipping fast.

Then the flame of the candle sprang again to life, and he could vaguely see again the inside of the room at the other side of the universe.

He was no longer alone. He tried and finally focused his eyes on her. She, the Seventh Sister, Sister Anjei was sitting there on the red rug and facing him, with the bowl of water and lit candle between them.

She wore a white and gold robe that covered her all over. All he could see was her head, neck, and a little portion of her wrists and hands.

Her hands were small and well kept, the fingernails were not long or painted. On the third finger of her left hand she wore a wide gold wedding band. That was the extent of the jewellery she wore on her hands, not even a wrist watch.

As with the little man at the door, he had no idea how old, or young she might be. Her complexion was very much like that of an American Indian, and her hair was long and black as a thousand midnights.

She said nothing and allowed him time to get a good look at her. While the intense stare of her dark eyes were at first unnerving, he suddenly wanted to confess all his sins to her, and beg forgiveness. Until that feeling was washed away by the tears that flowed freely down his face and dropped onto the envelopes he was clutching close to his chest.

Still she remained aloof and silent. Oh, she was beautiful. She was ugly, she was old and young. She was a saviour and a destroyer.

Her black hair was worn in the traditional Ethiopian fashion, corn rows or tightly braided to cover the head like a cap, and the ends left loose. There was absolutely no makeup marring her face.

Delta felt as tiny and insignificant as a grain of sand.

Until, all of a sudden he felt that he could command the elements of nature, command the storms, the lightning, the hurricanes.

The pain in his legs went away, and he was refreshed in the sure knowledge of himself.

She was sitting in a posture which seemed like Yogi fashion with her hands folded in front of her and her eyes were married to his eyes. Finally she spoke to him. He almost jumped with the difference in her voice as to that which he expected.

Her voice was sweet and mellow, a rare quality and blend, a lilting musical flow of distinct words that was in the true dialect of the people of Dahomey.

'Roosevelt Lincoln Washington, RW, aka Delta Sonny. Son of Jessie and Cleofus, grandson of Buddy Washington. You may call me Mambo if you wish to do so.

'Young man, before I begin the sacrament I must ask you if you have had sex with a woman within the last seven days?'

'No.'

She answered, before he could say a word. 'You see, I must ask that question, even though I would be a poor priestess if I didn't already know the answer before I ask you. On the other hand, the question does provide me with a sure fire method to know if you would lie to me. You wouldn't lie to me, would you?'

That time she waited for his answer.

'No ma'am, I surely would not lie to you.'

There was a long pause before she spoke again, 'Delta, that's the name you prefer. You can relax your grip on the essentials you have brought all the way from Chicago to me. And do tell me what you would have me do to Jewel Thomas, your sworn Enemy, and ex-lover. Would you have me give you the life force from her body. The wind from her lungs. The motivation from her legs, or the sight from her eyes. Would you be satisfied for me to turn her into a common house fly?'

'Ma'am, Mambo, I really don't want you to hurt her, certainly not to take her life. No, all I want is for you to please make her leave me and my family alone. That's all.'

'Delta, with the essence of her that you have in those envelopes, I

142

can kill her and you will be rid of her for ever. Do you fully understand that?'

'Yes, ma'am, I do and I still say to you I don't want to hurt her.'

'Then son of Jessie, I will do what is best for you. And I tell you true, if you had asked for her life, I would have turned you out. But as it is, now I'm sure where your heart is placed, be so kind and pass me what you collected from her locker in the police station.

'Pass the envelopes across the top of the bowl of holy water to me.'

She took the envelopes and carefully laid them along the edge of the bowl so they wouldn't fall into the water. From somewhere within or without the room on the other side of the universe came the gentle throbbing of the sacred drums.

The ritual invocation performed by her was short and still to the sound of the distant drums rolling to a rhythm that was so beautiful, he tried to remember how it went.

From the folds of her great cloak or robe, she removed two flat stones, both with one flat smooth side, and one side that was slightly convex and carved with mystic signs and symbols. The stones were round and about the same size as the top of a quart mason or fruit jar, and about an inch and a half thick.

Silently she placed one of the stones on the rug near her and with the flat side facing up. Next she took the top envelope, tore it open and poured the contents on to the stone. The same procedure was repeated with each envelope. The hair, dry skin and toe nail rested on the face of the upturned stone all together.

The flat face of the other stone was placed on top of the collected items and the other stone. From somewhere she produced a small piece of parchment and placed the stones on it so as not to lose any parts of the collection. Then she picked them up together and while whispering something that Delta couldn't really hear, she moved the stones in the same circular fashion that people have been grinding grain into meal, for years, and years.

Three times she stopped grinding and dipped the fingers of her left hand into the water and sprinkled some of it on the stones, and some on Delta.

The flame of the candle flickered. The sacred drums beat louder.

The items he brought were ground into a coarse powder, and she poured that powder into one of the already used envelopes, folded the open end down carefully and passed it across the water back to Delta.

'Take what is in this envelope back to Chicago, and spread it on the ground, or in such a location that she will have to walk over it at least one time.

'And it shall be done.

'You, son of Jessie, Delta Sonny, there is no charge for my services. Because you were sent to me first by Mama Zula, my teacher, and Mama Le Beaux, my student. On your way back to Chicago you will pass near one that is come to ride the wind, and I am not worthy to wash her feet.

'Go now! And walk easy in the sure knowledge that your enemy will trouble you no more...

'You are free of her, and because you were merciful, I have been merciful to her. However, my mercy does not extend to her two minions who have raped our women, before their sloppy attempt on Willie Mae. Those two are also murderers of the foulest degree. Their last victim was an old lady who they choked to death solely for her Social Security cheque so they could feed the big monkeys on their backs. Their asses are mine. Go now, go.'

The flame of the candle went out.

Her fading voice echoed in the bare room. 'Oh, I really do like your style of the old Blues. Specially the way you do "Devil in the Woodshed". Your recording contract will come to you soon, and it will be all that you hoped for.'

The candle flame sprang back to life. Delta was alone in the room, the Seventh Sister, Mama Loa, Mambo, was gone and leaving absolutely nothing there to indicate that she only seconds past sat before him.

No, there was one small item that said the high priestess was there. The torn and refolded white envelope which he held tightly in his hand. That was real.

And he clearly heard the bar being drawn on the door behind him, before the door swung open and was held by that little old white-haired man of undetermined age. He could see that the little man also held his shoes and socks in readiness.

Carefully he struggled to his feet, and started for the open door. That's when he noticed for the first time that not only did the room have no windows, but there was only one door, which was the door he was walking towards, and that door was barred from the outside.

Now how did she enter and leave the room?

After putting his socks and shoes back on, he gave the old man the wad of money he brought for that purpose. That he brought to Sister Anjei.

The little man smiled and returned the money to him. However, Delta put the money on the top of a nearby table, and asked that the money be given to the hungry and poor.

The little man smiled again, and nodded his head in approval of Delta's wish.

After leaving Mama Le Beaux and New Orleans, he rode the City to Jackson, and took a Hound to Belzoni. Once there, he carefully explained everything to his mother. They broke bread together, and he went back to Jackson, and from there up to Chicago.

When he walked into his own home, he just had to feel the partly folded envelope again for the umpteenth time. At supper he assured Wil and Mama Carter that the nightmare was at an end.

'But I won't be Blue always, cause the sun gon shine in my back door some day.'

*   *   *

In the very early hours of that day, around two-thirty in the morning, and after catching the front door to the building open, when a very drunk couple staggered in, he came silently to the front door of Jewel's apartment, checked the hall both ways, then he sprinkled the tiny bit of coarse powder, the spell, about half way between the left and right sides of the door frame. That way it would be impossible for Jewel not to pass over the small amount of powder.

Once the contents of the envelope was poured in a line from left to right, and near the floor, it was quite impossible to see that it was there.

Satisfied that the spell, which was really a curse, was in place, Delta went back home to a peaceful night's sleep.

That event took place on a Wednesday morning.

Thursday morning the Chicago newspapers carried a short story about an event that took place on the West Side, late Wednesday evening. Their stories went something like this:

Police woman shoots two men after they tried to rob her at gunpoint. One of Chicago's first coloured female officers, who was in plainclothes at the time of the incident, shot and killed two known criminals when they tried to rob her, she said.

Witnesses said they observed both men approach Officer Jewel Thomas near the mouth of an alley. At first they seemed to be on friendly terms, then an argument broke out.

One of the men was overheard to yell, 'Give me the damn money', or 'Give me our damn money. We want it right now or you gonna be dead ass dead!'

That's when one of the men attempted to grab the officer. The other man, the one with a patch over his eye, seemed to be going for a weapon.

Officer Thomas pulled her service revolver, and shot both men dead.

After the shooting, she told reporters that she would be leaving Chicago and going to New York or California for good.

You know, before Jewel left Chicago, she and Delta had the occasion to actually meet face to face. And you know what? She smiled at him, acted like she never saw him before in her life. There was absolutely no sign in her face or eyes that she recognised him.

There really was another way . . .

Chapter 22

Let It Roll

Wil's parents came to spend the weekend with them on the special occasion of the arrival of Wil's younger sister, who was moving from Birmingham, Alabama, which was the family's original home, to live with Wil and Delta.

Now Sarah, that was Wil's sister's name, was going to move in with them and take care of the baby. That way Wil could go back to work and school, Delta could continue on with his career, Mother Carter could go back home to take care of her husband, Simeon. Plus, it was good for Sarah, as she wanted to come to Chicago, but she didn't want to move in with her mother and father.

Sarah moved right on into the family with ease and soon she got to know little Jasmine. They named their baby Jasmine, 'because she was so sweet, and was the flower of their lives'.

So it was that the Washington family began the slow process of trying to heal the wounds inflicted by Jewel, the bad penny.

But you know, sometimes it's the little things that fester into the big things, which more than often have the bad habit of coming back to haunt us.

The wound was already festering. And over the period of the next few years Willie Mae would carefully assemble the pieces of the puzzle regarding that unknown-to-her and almost-faceless assailant who set her up, and directed the attack on her. The person who stole her baby and put a dead rat in the bed to replace her child.

Without her husband's knowledge, and because she was a strong, intelligent, and a persistent woman, she would in time correctly assemble the pieces of the puzzle, including her husband's involvement with her attacker.

But, until that time, the skeleton was firmly entrenched in the bedroom closet.

Delta's first night back at the Little Queen of Clubs was a most rewarding time, because the place was packed with his fans and people who liked him and his music; that was their way of welcoming him back home.

Oh, it was all so wonderful. LD was there on the drums, and Crazy Willie was doing himself proud playing backup. The little fellow who played the best harp in the business was there to help welcome Delta Sonny back home, to the Blues.

After a warm-up medley, Delta got comfortable in his old chair which he sat in the centre front of the bandstand. The microphone was positioned just right, and the small spotlight was adjusted to place him almost in its shadow. He wore his old floppy black hat, which was coming to be accepted as his trademark. All along with the common dress that was almost traditional to the Mississippi delta.

The present-whenever-possible piece of plywood on the floor close to his right foot was also properly positioned and just waiting to echo the beat.

The crowd became suddenly quiet without being told to do so. They waited in rapt anticipation for him to get ready, and for what his first number would be.

Delta looked out at the sea of expectant and friendly faces, some new, but mostly familiar faces, that always kept coming back.

Once again he was among friends, his people, the people of Little Delta. He could actually feel the real Mississippi delta, and the love that went along with it.

Lord, lord, let the good times roll.

One, one two, one . . . '

Lord I'm a po boy long, long ways from home.
I ain't got no body to call my own.
I'm broke and I'm hungry, I ain't got a dime
Every po boy get this way sometime.

Have mercy! You could just feel the Blues go rippling through the crowd. So much so, that the crowd began to rock in time with the rhythm and beat, all backed up with the sweetest harp in the city of Chicago.

Some folk began to moan, and some folk was just saying 'Yes, Lord, yes, Lord'. If you have ever picked cotton in the delta. If you have ever walked behind a big grey mule pulling a plow. If you have ever heard the mournful cry of hound dogs chasing coon.

Then you will know what I'm trying to say.

When Po Boy was done he flowed smoothly right on into 'One Dime Blues', and 'Make me a Pallet Down on Your Floor'. By that time Delta had developed a way of presenting his songs so that they told a story. Sometimes the story was about travelling, sometimes it was about a lost love, a no-good cheating woman, gambling, or sometimes it was just about the story of the Blues.

That night, he was telling the true story about a poor boy who was a long way from home, and out there in the real world trying to pay his dues. That Po Boy met a dirty lying cheating woman who gave him a one-way ticket to Parchman.

The crowd just sat or stood, and listened to old Delta preach the Blues. Oh, the Little Queen of Clubs was like a Baptist Church on Sunday morning, and Delta was preaching.

He moved them on up a little higher with such great numbers as:

'Travellin' Blues'
'You Upset My Mind'
'You Don't Have To Go'
'Honest I Do'
'C C Rider'
'Stack-O-Lee Blues'
'Parchman Farm Blues'
'John Henry'

'Big Boss Man'
'When Can I Change My Clothes'
'Blue Midnight'
And ending with his usual 'Devil in the Woodshed'.

Now that's pretty much the way he did the first set, before they took a breather. You see, what he did was to start from the time he left home, to his meeting Jewel which was characterised by Jimmy Reed's 'You Upset My Mind'. Then on to Parchman Farm, the chain gang and driving steel, like old John Henry. And when he was able to change his clothes and get out of prison.

'Blue Midnight' was the start of the new day of his life, and his way of letting Little Walter do his thing. Oh, to be sure, like always, Delta tried to honour as many of the all-time great Bluesmen as possible, whenever he performed.

The last number he did that night was 'Precious Lord Take My Hand'. Everyone stood up and joined in the singing of that fine old Gospel song.

Some of the other Bluesmen of Chicago came to sit in with Delta that night and because of that special occasion, the Little Queen of Clubs was also the home of the Blues for that night, and point in time.

I tell you there were a lot of misty eyes, and a lot of country hearts that went on back down home to the Mississippi delta. Even if it was only for a short time.

Delta Sonny was back, the real and true country Blues was back. And he was the prophet, the oracle, the true Bluesman. Surely by that time he had earned the right to stand alone, a true Bluesman in his own right.

'Cause Dear Lord he had surely, 'Been up on the Mountain of Pain'.

He didn't stop playing and singing, he couldn't stop. The enchanting power of the Blues was upon him, and that enchantment flowed out like the mighty Mississippi and took everyone along with the flow.

He looked back at LD, Crazy Willie, Little Walter, and the others who just slid on in and he saw it on their faces. They were all with him.

That's why when they finally stood and sang:

Precious Lord take my hand,
Lead me on, let me stand,

the sun of the new day was shining through the windows of the club.

Oh, you know something very odd happened while Delta was doing 'Devil in the Woodshed'. When the number was over, he said into the mike, 'Mambo, that was for you.'

And the entire lighting system of the club did something that never happened before. The lights blinked off and on seven distinct times...

Chapter 23

Ups and Downs

The very nice white lady shook his hand, and told him she wanted to sign him to her record label. That if he signed with her, 'they would surely be able to work something out which would be good for both him, and her'.

Plus she promised the contract would be adjustable so he could bring along LD and Crazy Willie. That part really did make him happy, 'cause too often the men who work alongside the guy who gets a break are left to fend for themselves. Well, no way would that happen to the people who had supported him for so long.

Oh, to be sure, Delta knew who she was, and what her offer meant to him, and his two best friends. Both LD and Willie fully deserved to be there when the cream came to the top.

Hell, yes, he would sign!

That was when he found out that she was in the club his first night back after getting rid of his bad penny. And she returned on at least three other nights. Funny, he didn't see her either time. The owner of the club knew all about it, but promised her that he wouldn't tell Delta. Leastwise till she was ready to offer him and his group a contract.

So then, after all those years of doing what he loved best, and waiting in the rear, old Delta Sonny was finally getting the chance to play centre stage. He was going to have his own recording label, which I might add was one of the top labels in the entire music industry.

> We're going to raise a ruckus tonight.

> Must I holler, or must I shake em on down.

Jimmy went along with them to the contract signing, and after that was over they went to 51st Street and had chop suey, and later that night they went to the Pershing ballroom and finished the night off at the Club DeLisa.

When he and Wil got home both Sarah and Jasmine were asleep, so they went to bed still very happy about the fact that soon there would be record jackets and labels all over the country with Delta's name on them.

> I'm so glad I done got over,
> I done got over at last.

When the day arrived that he was to go into the recording studios downtown he was ready for Freddy. Of course he had already arranged for one of the new guys on Maxwell Street to sit in with them. He surely didn't forget to give someone else a hand, just like he was given.

Two other Bluesmen were also there, but they were already on top, and there to lend him support, and their expertise.

That was the time of the full beginning of the large $33^1/_3$ record disc so his first album was cut and pressed in that format. The title of the album was *Delta to Delta*, and the album cover featured a large photo of him and his best girl, Fanny Mae, his guitar.

The new $33^1/_3$ formatted disc was chosen so as to go with the flow, and what was new. Also there was the increasingly popular Hi-Fi single units, and component systems which were designed to complement the larger records, or was it the other way around?

Anyway, the record producers also recorded on to the 45 rpm single discs with the large hole, all the cuts from his large disc. That way his songs would appear on the jukeboxes, be suitable for the radio DJs, and of course be available to those who had only the old players and the 45 adapters. Those for whom a nickel was a nickel.

By that time the old 78 rpm phonograph records were being turned out to pasture, and becoming remaining traces of yesterday.

Well, it goes without saying, Delta Sonny's first album and singles were a hit. Almost overnight, and soon as the distributors could supply the demand. You could hear the voice of Delta Sonny, Fanny Mae and his harp, all over the Little Delta. On the West Side, Gary, and just about everywhere the Blues was in demand.

His first thought was to send a copy of his first album, and some singles, home to his mother. But after giving the idea more thought, he decided to *take* them to her.

He would personally put them in her hands, that was the way it should be. And Wil was quick to agree. So they arranged to drive down home to Belzoni, and do a little visiting at the same time.

During the long drive down, they had time to talk openly and seriously about their new-found prominence. Of course it took only a short while before they got on down to where the rubber meets the road. Wil pointed out that since the incidents and attacks stopped he had spent or devoted almost all his time to the club. Sure, she understood that he may be trying to forget the horrible experience.

But she felt that he spent entirely too much time away from her and Jasmine.

So it was that during the conversation he made the sad discovery that his wife wasn't as happy with their marriage as he thought she was. His success which had taken so long to come was viewed as almost just another day. That the attack in the alley on her body, and the following incidents, still caused her to tremble and wonder.

Right then and there he wanted to lay it all out to her so she could see and hear the whole sad story. To get the skeleton out of the closet. To get that load which was killing him off his heart and shoulders.

But listening to how she said what she said, and watching the expression on her face as she said what she said, all that told him the time was not right. Even in those close moments, and within the quiet confines of his Roadmaster.

The time wasn't right.

Frankly, old Delta saw and felt something else. His Delta survival senses detected a dead cat on the line. And his heart sank to a new low. It was all there right before him, but he chose to ignore it, saying to himself that he was over-reacting, that his first thought was wrong.

That his bad feeling was brought on by his failing to realise, or take into consideration just how deep the wounds of Jewel's attacks on Wil really were.

Was the damage irreparable? Was Jewel still going to have her revenge after all? He had to think. So he tried to change the conversation. To talk about things that he had a better handle on.

Sure, he made it up in his mind that he would most certainly spend as much time with his family as possible, and if that wasn't enough he would just quit and come home.

You know, it's a sad fact, but there is a whole world of good men out there who try too hard to make it better for their families by working harder and harder. And the sad thing is their very trying is in fact killing them, the marriage, and family.

Once home they successfully put on the face that said everything was all right. Jasmine was having the time of her life. And of course Jessie and Percy were giving their little granddaughter all the love a little girl could handle.

During the second day they were home, he took Wil to the cemetery at Shady Grove to pay his respects to those of his family, including Mama Zula, sleeping quietly there. After spending some quiet moments in solitude they walked back past the old house he was born in. Then they walked on down to the bottom, to Mama Zula's house.

It was hard to believe, but the house was still empty. Nobody would even go close, even in the broad daylight. For some unexplained reason it surely did look lived in, like she was still living there. Jessie said the old boss man sent some men with gasoline down there to burn the old place down to the ground.

But when the men ran home the only thing that was burned was them. Old Frank Plummer's hair never did grow back. Since that time they tried again two or three times and all attempts ended in failure. So the old man said...

While they were standing in the front yard, and he was showing her the remnants of the Klan's one and only attack on the old lady, Wil suddenly grabbed his arm in sudden fright.

She swore to God that she saw an old woman smiling at her from the window. And then a big dark cat ran around the corner of the house.

'Honey, let's get away from here, right now!'

While they were getting ready to come back home, Wil and Jessie were talking about some totally unrelated subject, when Jessie let slip something that tore the hell out of Delta's story that during the time right after the attacks she was sick and he had to go home.

Like most lies, that one was out in the light. He had the sincere hope that what his Mother said went unnoticed, but we know it didn't.

On the drive back home, they each avoided talking about what happened to them, who the woman in the alley was, why she was attacked, and such things.

Of course just because they didn't talk about it, surely didn't mean that it wasn't still right there between them. Delta felt sick. He knew something was between them, and that something wasn't all that happened to them. He thought old Time would heal, and ease the pain.

While Willie Mae was silently remembering the ghostly face of the woman she saw in the window, Mama Zula, she didn't tell her husband that she saw the woman's eyes most clearly, and that those eyes were definitely accusing her of...

You know, there is an old saying that goes something like this: time will heal all wounds, and cause you to forget the bad times and remember only the good.

Well, there's something that you should know: that old saying isn't always true.

Specially when Wil wasn't about to forget, 'cause she really didn't want to forget. So far as she was concerned the mysterious woman got clean away with all she did. Sure the attacks suddenly stopped, and he assured her it wouldn't happen again. But.

She didn't understand the why for it all, and poor old Delta was scared to tell her. Talk about a sticky situation. What would you have done? If you were he?

Meantime, Delta's career moved along nicely. See, that was the time that there was some discovering the real Blues and the people who made the Blues possible. Now some folks laboured under the misconception that the Blues was only a black folks' thing. Clearly all the singers of the Blues were coloured at that time. Black or African American now.

Well, you see, there was most definitely a line between coloured folks' music and white folks' music. Or perhaps that line was more a wall.

A wall that was erected to prevent the passage of low-class coloured music from crossing over and polluting the high-class music of the blue bloods.

Sure, I know that now it's hard to believe, but those were also the times when some misguided people felt that the country Blues was low class. That if you wanted to join or maintain the status quo you didn't listen to the Blues of the old country Bluesmen, but rather listened to the music of the whites.

Even though it was necessary for him to keep working hard, if he wanted to live decently, and have some of the things he had always dreamed of having, he had to adjust his time so he could be there with his family every possible minute.

And he made it a point to tell Wil that he loved her, and to be a real father to his little daughter, who was growing up to be very smart, and a real beautiful child.

One might think there was a lot of money coming to him now that he was making records. But again, that wasn't true. The money he made at the club, from his records, and playing special occasions certainly didn't put him into the wealthy or rich bracket.

No, sir. Delta was no different than the hundred of other Bluesmen in the Chicago area who had achieved some degree of prominence. There just wasn't that much money out there. Not even for the superstars.

However, and not to complain, the Washingtons made it OK. Wil was studying to become a doctor, they were buying a home, and Jasmine was in school, and doing well.

Because of her school and work, Wil was away from home for a lot of time, just like it once was with Delta.

When the shoe was on the other foot he could surely appreciate how Wil felt when he was working so hard and spending so much time away from his family.

To tell the truth, old Delta couldn't shake the feeling that old Trouble was coming to meet him. Often he felt the presence of Mama Zula like she was trying to warn him...

Chapter 24

Friday the 13th Child

The years passed quickly. And Delta Sonny the Bluesman, husband, and father rode the waves of his success with dignity, pride and humility. And did all with equal vigour and perfectly balanced, so that all who knew him respected him for the man and the Bluesman that he surely was.

Oh, and Jewel did just as Sister Anjei, the Seventh Sister, Mama Loa, and Mambo, told Delta she would do. That is, she would never return to bother him again. And Jewel did just that, exactly.

More years passed, Delta and his family lived in their modest home in the Hyde Park area on the South Side, and not too far from the Lake. Wil was by that time a doctor of medicine with her residency at Cook County over, and she being back to Provident a full doctor. Jasmine was doing very well in school, and promising to follow in her mother's footsteps.

Now that was during those troubled years when there was a landmark and history making movement in progress. The march was on towards freedom and equality.

That march or movement was initiated by a wonderful lady who refused to get up and give her seat on the bus to a man, simply because that man was white.

You might say that she fired the silent shot that was heard round the world.

159

Because of that shot conditions in the South, and mainly Mississippi, worsened, and Delta tried again to get his mother to come to him in Chicago. She refused, again, saying that 'they would hold onto what they had, that she wouldn't be run off'.

That particular period of time was also the time when Delta chose to finally get the load of the 'great lie' off his mind, heart and shoulders.

He felt that enough years had passed that he could safely, and without hurting her, tell Wil all about Who and Why and the final results of that period of their lives which had caused such a turmoil. He would also explain to her why he lied to her, and why he kept it locked up in his heart for so long.

So it was, on the night before the day that he had set aside to tell her, and just before he left the club, Roy, the bartender, gave him a plain white envelope, which had only the name Delta, scrolled in a bold feminine hand across the front.

When Delta asked who the envelope was from, Roy could only tell him that 'A man that I never saw in here before gave the letter to me, and told me to be sure and give it to you. I told him he could wait and give it to you himself. But he said he was in a hurry 'cause he had to go all the way back to Algeria.

'You know, that's funny, 'cause that guy sure didn't look like no Arab to me. Specially him being dressed all in black like he was. Come to think of it, you know, I didn't see him come in, or leave.' Roy sounded just a little worried as he spoke.

Delta's hands were already shaking as he took the envelope. He already knew there was only one person in all the world that envelope could be from. Roy went to finish his nightly inventory, and other routines before going home for the night.

And Delta looked around to ensure he was alone, before he tore the envelope open, to find a single plain white sheet of paper which bore a precise handwritten message.

The message read like this:

> The truth is a lie,
> A lie is the truth,
> The truth to date,

160

Is the truth too late.
What is to be you can't hide,
Let it ride, let it ride...'

The cryptic message was signed simply: Devil in the Woodshed.

Of course, you, me, and Delta know who that little message was from, don't we?

But you know, what should have happened, didn't happen.

You see, Delta had been preparing Wil a few days for what he had to tell her. And he felt that he had already said too much to her to back down. So, he decided to ignore the message and go ahead and tell her.

Besides he was dragging in the dirt, and his shoulders hurt from carrying that terrible load for so many years. Not to mention the guilt he felt for not telling her when it happened.

It was a Friday morning, Jasmine was off to school, and Wil had the day off, all in all a perfect day to let it all hang out.

'Honey, now that we are alone, and we both have time, I want you to tell me all that you know about what happened to us that time, and I want you to begin with the attack in the alley. I can't wait any longer!' Wil begin by asking. And her approach clearly took the moment away from him. Her tone of voice, and expression on her face, told him that she wasn't to be denied.

He took a long breath, let some of it out, and began at the beginning, starting with that night long ago in Piney Woods, Mississippi. Then he slowly and not missing a thing brought her up to the last time that he saw Jewel.

You know, even before he was finished, he accepted the fact that he should have listened to the message and let it ride. Still it was too late to turn back, he was already out there. On that long lonesome road all by himself.

There were too many rivers already crossed.

When he finally finished what he had to say, the quietness in the room was so loud that it hurt his ears. She just sat there staring off into space, oh, it seemed she sat that way for a good two to three minutes before she spoke.

161

'Now tell me again why you waited all these years to tell me the truth?'

'Honestly and truly, I felt deep in my heart that it was best to wait, and not to tell you it was Jewel when I found out that it really was her.

'Wil, you had enough on your heart, and if you are thinking that I thought you wouldn't understand if I told you, then you are surely right, that's exactly what I thought.

'I was so scared that you might blame me, that I might lose you. Wil, I lied to you when I said later that I didn't know who the woman in the alley was. I really didn't know who it was till I followed, and got a close look at her, and that was after the attack in the alley.

'Baby, I'm so sorry I didn't tell you the whole story before now, and you know what? I'm still scared.'

To his great surprise, she seemed to accept his full account of what happened, or as he knew it. She seemed to take it all in her stride.

Sure she waited a long time before she spoke, but then she was digesting what she heard and formulating her reply, and that was a wise thing to do. He felt that everything was going to be all right. Maybe he did right to go ahead and tell her. Was the message wrong?

'I'm glad you didn't kill her, or have her killed. To do that would have made you as low as she was. And I can understand that you were trying to protect me.' She put special emphasis on the words, 'to protect me'. 'But I can't help but to feel that you really should have told me.'

> Trouble in mind I'm blue but I won't be blue always
> Cause the sun gon shine in my back door someday.
> I'm going to lay my head on some lonesome railroad iron,
> And let that two-nineteen pacify my mind.

Now you know, it was exactly seven months and seven days later and on a Friday morning that Willie Mae asked old Delta for a divorce.

She told him in a very frank manner and tone that she was leaving him, that she didn't love him no more. And, she was taking Jasmine with her, also she would be out of the house before nightfall.

'Oh, baby, you don't have to go.' The words of Jimmy Reed's mournful tune crept into his mind and heart. Above the sound and echo of those hurtful words. His knees buckled and he had to sit down, before he fell down.

> Don't tell me where you come from,
> Just tell me where you going.

Have you ever heard a guy talk about 'what he would do if that ever happened to him'? Now some people will swear to you, 'Man, I would kill her, I would do this and that.'

Well, let me say it right here, you don't know what you would do till after it happens to you. Then and only then can you tell what you did.

First off, he cried like a little baby. He couldn't hold back the tears, they just flooded right on down his face. He tried to tell himself that he was only dreaming. That he would wake up and she would be rolling in his arms.

But the pain in his heart told him it was real. Wil was saying those things to him. He heard her right the first time. He heard a pitiful squeaking voice begging her:

'Baby, please don't go!'

At no time did he even think of hurting her. At no time did he feel malice toward her. Instead he wanted to hold her. To make the awful pain go away. 'Wil, I love you. Baby, what have I done for you to treat me this way? Baby, I ain't too proud to beg.'

> Come back baby, baby please don't go
> Cause the way I love you you'll never know,
> Come back baby,
> Let's talk it over one more time.

163

My heart's full of sorrow my eye's full of tears
Cause we been together for so many years.
Come back baby, let's talk it over one more time.

She already had her things packed, and told him that Jasmine was in school, but that she was with her mother, and wouldn't be coming home again.

Delta told her that he would have to fight her for his daughter. He really didn't want to fight her, but he would, that he wouldn't let her just take his only child away from him.

Oh, if he thought she had already hurt him, sweet Jesus, he was in for an earthshaking awaking.

'Wil, are you planning to take my child way from me too?' The sad thought invaded his mind, and was like salt in an open wound.

'Cause if that's what you plan on doing, then I will have to fight you for her. Oh, I won't contest a divorce. If you don't love me, and no longer want to be with me, that's one thing. But if you are planning to take my daughter...'

'Well, since you brought it up, I guess there is no better time for me to tell you that you are not Jasmine's father...

'When I met you I was going with the man that is her father. But during that time we were split up over something stupid. Now, I want you to know that I really didn't keep on seeing him after I started to go out with you.

'But because we worked so close together at the hospital, it was impossible for me not to see him on a daily basis. And shortly after you and I were married, one night we had duty together, and it just happened.

'Delta, the truth is that Doctor Orin A. La Salle the third is actually Jasmine's real father. He is the man that I will marry soon as our divorce is final.

'Honey, I'm real sorry. I just didn't know how to tell you before, and like you once said, "after I didn't tell you soon as I was sure, I was afraid to tell you later."'

BOOM...

Friday the 13th Child,
Mama nearly died in pain.
Friday the 13th Child
There's a rabbit dying on the road.

His world dropped out from under his feet. He hung suspended somewhere between heaven and hell. Somewhere between reality, and that which wasn't.

His mind stopped working, and he sat there totally numb and temporarily brain dead. Poor Delta was only aware of his erratic heart beating.

Willie Mae, his dear and devoted wife of many years, had in fact destroyed him in place. No man, no matter what the situation might be, should have to suffer such a wound.

Please write my Mother and tell her to Pray for me,
Cause I'm going down slow.

Delta just sat there slowly rocking back and forward, and humming softly.

Well my health is failing me
And I'm going down slow.
Tell my Mama to look for my clothes home,
And if she don't see no body, all she can do is moan.

Oh I tell you, that poor boy was pitiful. He was just staring straight ahead and looking down on the world from his lofty perch. He was oblivious to the surroundings of his own home.

In reality, he was sitting right there at his kitchen table, his hands together almost as if in prayer. He continued to rock back and forward. And all the while he was sadly moaning the heartbreaking melody to the enchanting 'Devil in the Woodshed'.

Now to tell it like it was, old Willie Mae was real close to flipping her wig. She was sweating like hell, and her mouth was dry as a powder house. She was trying desperately to shut out the heartbreaking sounds of his moaning, and even though the sound

165

coming from him was just a little above a whisper.

When the melody of 'Devil in the Woodshed' reached her ears, it crashed into her brain like the blast of the whistle of a lonesome freight train on its way to hell.

She was attempting to grab a few more personal things, as she hurriedly cleared out. But, all her haste and efforts were in vain. 'Cause no matter where she went in the house, she could still most plainly hear him.

Wil grabbed her last bag, and ran to the front door, still trying to escape the strange moaning sounds of his humming. She tried to open the door. But the door refused to open. Something was holding it shut.

Course, by that time the true meaning of her awful deed was seeping into her muddled mind. And she couldn't shut off the seeping.

She tried the door again. Still it refused to budge, and there was no earthly reason why that damn door shouldn't open. But it didn't.

And to top that off, suddenly standing there before her, between her and the door, was a sight that shook her to the core. She would have to change panties soon as possible.

There standing serenely before her was an old woman.

The face of the old woman standing there before her was the same face that she saw smiling at her from the window of that old empty house on Lightcap's.

She was looking at a one hundred per cent ghost, and she damn well knew that one thing for certain.

'Oh my, oh my God, my dear God,' Wil screamed, as she broke for the kitchen, in a futile effort to get some comfort from the only other living being in the house.

But, alas, old Delta was out of it. He didn't seem to take note of her even being there. Let alone her screaming and pointing towards the living room.

'Stop it! Shut up, damn it. Oh please, I'm sorry, I didn't mean for it to be this way. Don't you see, now that I'm a doctor and no longer just a nurse, it ain't right that my husband is only a country Blues singer.

166

'I should be married to a man of class, a professional person like me. You are a good man, I'll give you that, but you are country, I, I, I'm sorry, sorry. Please make that mean old woman go away, please!' she screamed.

But you know what? Old Delta was way past hearing her words, and he just sat there humming. She fell down on her knees beside him, and begged his forgiveness. She even asked him to forget the whole thing.

But he still didn't hear a word she said.

When that realisation struck her, and along with the tears and fears of the old woman by the front door, she decided to leave her stuff on the living-room floor, and escape with her butt; she could always send someone back to get her personal belongings.

She scrambled for the kitchen door, grabbed the knob, and that's right, you guessed it, that door was also locked, and/or mysteriously refused to open.

That time the old woman materialised in the most distant corner of the kitchen, so as not to push Wil's mind that last-minute distance. And as she spoke her voice came clear and without malice:

'Hear me, Woman who is not a woman. And listen well to what I have to say. The River is long, and the water is cold. You will swim before you will sink, and your sins will hold you down, before you grow old.

'Go now, you "lady of class". Go to your lover, and perhaps father of your child. But before you do, I want you to see and know that you have really hurt a good man, a man who really loved you.

'The man you are running to, the good Doctor La Salle, the third, is not the man you think he is, or want him to be. But then you will find that out yourself, and you will scream to the wind about what you have done here today. Oh yes, you will see it as it comes right on back to you.

'I also want you to know that it is I who have made it so that Delta's present condition is only a temporary one. He will come around soon enough, and I want you gone before he does.'

The old lady's last words were heavy with sadness, and even Wil knew that the ghost would not harm her, that it was she who had harmed herself.

The kitchen doors opened by themselves. First the wood door and then the screen door; they stood wide open, held by invisible hands.

The old woman was gone.

And, Willie Mae, the former Mrs Washington, Doctor Washington, and Lady of Class, ran out to the street and down the block, to where a handsome man in a great big Cadillac waited.

> Oh Black Betty's in the bottom,
> Let your hammer ring,
> Black Betty's in the bottom
> Let your hammer ring.

> She'll bring you here and she'll leave you
> Let your hammer ring.

Delta sat there alone for well over two hours before he suddenly snapped out of the condition imposed on him by the good spirit.

Now that condition had saved his hide, 'cause you see when Wil told him about her good doctor lover, that was the time for her to die. But Mama Zula didn't want it that way. So she stepped in, and saved him from himself.

There were a lot of things the spirits could do, and a lot of things they couldn't do.

Once he was back in this cruel old world of hurts and pain, he sat there alone just thinking about what happened to him, and wishing.

Then he got up, made himself presentable, locked the house, leaving her bags where she dropped them, and he drove straight to Mama Carter's House.

After hearing his story they held each other, cried together, and later they cried some more. That was the very first time that Simeon told them some of what happened to him. Once they heard his story which took place at Buchenwald, Delta no longer felt it was the end of the world for him.

There's always someone who has a larger cross to carry than you have.

The divorce went without a hitch, there was no child support, and Wil didn't try to stick him with any alimony. He turned the house and everything in it over to Simeon and Mama Carter to sell for him. Everything at the Club was turned over to Crazy Willie and LD.

Once that was all taken care of, he took Fanny Mae and got into his car and headed south back to the Delta, Belzoni, and Jessie.

> I've told you my story,
> Sang my song
> Now you just about to leave me
> You know that's wrong.
> Bye bye baby, bye bye baby
> I won't be troubled no more.

Chapter 25

A New Day

He just didn't have the heart to go back to the Little Queen of Clubs. He couldn't stand the pained look of sympathy for him on the faces of his friends. By that time the whole Little Delta knew all the gruesome details of his shattered life.

More than once his friends told him to bring her down, when a woman does that to a man, she is in desperate need of killing. But not to just kill her, the good doctor should be brought down too.

He even had two offers by someone who would do the job, for free.

Willie and LD could handle things. Besides there was already a new Bluesman over on Maxwell Street, and that man had played with him at the club, and was accepted.

Let's face it, the Queen of Clubs, Willie, and LD would survive. They hadn't come all that way riding someone's coat tail.

He tried to hold up under the great strain, possibly the greatest strain of his whole life. To raise Jasmine up to be the most beautiful little girl in all the world. To cover her with his love and devotion. To look at her with such pride, his one and only child in his own image.

Then to have it all, and her, snatched away from him. To be told that she was not his child, his daughter, his own flesh and blood.

I know it's quite impossible for you, or anyone who hasn't been there, to have the slightest idea of how much pain old Delta felt.

You would have to stand in his shoes. And I wouldn't wish that on anyone.

Oh, how cruel the real world can be, and that was just for openers.

The fact plagued him that he never once thought that Willie Mae was even remotely capable of such a thing, of such cruelty, and to direct that cruelty to him.

Isn't it funny how those things between our legs control our lives, and often make us do things that are way beyond even our wildest imagination? About fifty per cent of all the homicides in a given area are tangible testimony to that fact.

Now some folk say it's done in the name of love, but we know better, don't we?

The beautiful memories of the many wonderful years they spent together, and the many nights they held each other. Those beautiful moments were all lies, all a charade.

And she didn't even stutter, when she lowered the boom on him.

Any man who says that he knows and understands women is either a fool, or he doesn't have a woman.

That thought crossed Delta's mind, and he pulled over on the shoulder of the highway. There was a road sign only a short distance away from where he stopped. The sign announced that he was in the vicinity of Indian Oaks.

His mind was on his fully loaded .38 resting under his seat. He could turn around and go back. Catch them somewhere and blow them away. And that would be that. Goodness knows he had the reason, and they had it coming.

It was only a short run back to the South Side, and he could set things right. He could bring her and Doctor Whatcha may call him, right on down front, permanently.

The appealing thought of dropping the good doctor's laundry was actually the turning point. You see, the good doctor could only do what Wil wanted him to do.

That night, she sure as hell messed those guys in the alley up, big time. And while they were holding her down, flat on her back. All that 'cause she didn't want them to have it.

So, if anyone deserved to be dropped, then that one was Willie

171

Mae. The good doctor was only the bone for the dog, when it happened.

Yes. It was Willie Mae who needed killing.

That line of thinking caused him to think of little Jasmine. If he took her mother out, or both her mother and father out, just where would that leave Jasmine?

Now if he really loved her, even after all that was said and done, and no matter what happened to him, if that Love was true love for Jasmine . . .

No! He couldn't do it, he couldn't make his used-to-be-daughter just another victim. Lord knows the black community of Chicago had more than its share of victims.

'What ever you do will come on back to you.'

Delta pulled back on the highway, and headed on down towards Kankakee and Champaign.

The trip from Chicago to Belzoni took old Delta seven weeks to make. It's not really clear what happened. He was OK till he passed Memphis, he remembers stopping for a hamburger, and gas. Then going on past the Mississippi State Line.

He made the quick decision to go through Holly Springs, and on down to Tupelo, 'cause he wanted to visit an old Bluesman that he knew there. Also he was hoping the diversion would be good for him, and he could sit and play some of the real old Blues with Uncle George Harper. Like they once did many years ago.

Uncle George was an old friend of Delta's grandfather. The old man was practically indestructible and truly a living legend in his own time. Folk said he was one hundred years old, and still could pick his age in cotton, which was a hundred pounds. That he could drink the average young man under the table, and make a young gal holler.

Well, Delta stayed there with Uncle George, and his under-thirty young wife. They did pick and sing to their hearts' content. Then Delta left early one morning heading for Grenada, and that's when time for him was interrupted.

What took place between the time he left Uncle George's place, and seven weeks later when he drove his battered and dusty new car up to his mother's house, is a complete mystery.

172

Delta had no idea about what happened, and probably would never be able to bring those weeks and time into focus. He blanked out plain and simple, or maybe it wasn't as plain and simple as one might think it was.

There is an old saying. 'What you don't know can't hurt you.' Is that really true?

He just sat there in the car, the motor still running. He was unable to get out, unable even to turn the ignition off.

Jessie heard the car come up, and when she saw who was driving it, she screamed in pain at the sight of her last and only son. And while rushing to the car, she called out 'Percy, come and help me quick!'

The terrible heart-stopping memories of that early morning when she found BC lying and dying on her front porch were almost too much to bear again.

Both she and Percy couldn't hold back the tears at the sickening sight that greeted them when she opened the car door. By the time Percy got there she had already shut off the motor.

He still wore the same clothes he was wearing when he left Uncle George's house in Tupelo. In a few words, Delta was filthy beyond words of description.

More than once he had relieved himself, without dropping his trousers. Oh, that boy stunk so bad that the odour from him would puke a buzzard off a gut wagon. The stench of old urine and faeces was overpowering.

His mother came to the correct conclusion. That the sad load Wil had thrown on his mind and heart was far too much for any man to bear, and old Delta had finally buckled under the strain.

The only visible indication that he was even partly aware of the fact that he was home came as they gently lifted him from the car. That's when great big tears rolled down his very dirty face. He knew that he was home.

Otherwise, he didn't say one word, not even a whimper or grunt. Seemed like he lost the ability, or desire to speak. Along with the ability to do most of the other things that a grown man could normally do.

Roosevelt Lincoln Washington, aka Delta Sonny, was again a

little baby child. All the way back to not being able to speak, or wipe his own butt.

All his money was gone; she found his wallet in the trunk of the car in the spare tyre well, the spare was missing. Some of his papers were strewn around in the trunk and on the floor, both rear and front.

Jessie specially looked under the driver's side of the front seat, and all through the car for his .38, but it was not to be found. The practically new Roadmaster Buick was a sad sight. It was all banged up, the right front fender had a permanent wrinkle in it, and there was what surely looked like a bullet hole in the trunk lid.

All his personal things were gone, the seat covers were ripped, torn, and covered with splotches of things caused by what? Even his shoes were missing, he was barefoot. Of course Fanny Mae, his harp, everything with the exception of his old battered black hat was gone. He had only the dirty filthy rags he was wearing, if one could really stretch the word wearing, on his body.

His mother steeled her heart, and did all the things that only a mother would do for her child. She washed him, put homemade salves on his open sores, and put him to bed.

Then she fed him, and when that was over she had to wipe his ass. And finally that wonderful woman that was his mother knelt down beside his bed and thanked the Good Lord for bringing her son back to her. Yes Lord.

> Precious Lord take my hand,
> lead me on, let me stand
> The Lord will make a way somehow.

She took his hand and prayed to God to give her the strength to fight off the evil of a no good woman, and old death who was just standing there and waiting.

Well, you know what? I think Jessie already had that strength she was asking God to give her, yes, it was all right there inside her. The proof of what I say was in the fact that she had survived that long in the Mississippi delta.

Which was no small feat if you have some knowledge of those times.

Without the precious love of his dear mother, Delta would have wound up out there in Shady Grove Cemetery, pushing up daisies, and that's for sure.

Instead she took his hand and led him back past the pillars of the land of the dead. She brought him back into this mean old world for the second time.

Lord, let your light shine on me so that I may be born again.

After more than three long months, and one bright Friday morning, old Delta spoke his first words since he came back home.

'Thank you, Mama, I love you so much, thank you...'

Simeon and Mama Carter came down to see him and they brought the sad news that he 'Wouldn't receive not one penny more from his recording contract because he defaulted, which broke his contract.' Fact was, the fine print was killing him.

He had only the few dollars that he had enough sense to give to Simeon to hold for him, plus some savings bonds he purchased, but the bonds were made out to him and Willie Mae.

By that time Delta was all the way back to normal.

Well, the grand old South, and more specifically the Mississippi delta that he once knew, was no more. That was the time of those hard changes. The feeling of change was in the very air, and no one could help but feel them changes.

The racists, bigots, and true red necks were doing their very best to keep their God, old Jim Crow, in power, on the throne of hate, and alive.

They were beating and killing both black and white people, in the lost cause of white supremacy. And they were showing their true yellow colours on the stage of the whole world through the media.

The whole wide world watched as they showed what cowards they really were when they unleashed the mad dogs, both the four-legged and two-legged kind, on old defenceless people, women, children and even babies.

And all that on world television.

175

Meantime, the march towards freedom continued. The marchers representing the people of the people of all races and ethnic backgrounds grew longer, and longer. And reaching all the way back to the Original Dream.

In the midst and throes of the changing times, Delta decided to go on the road again. Simeon bought him a new guitar and harp, Percy had already replaced his piece of board and he had an old neck piece there at the house, so he had everything he would need to once again become the Bluesman that he really was.

The Roadmaster had something wrong with its Dynaflow drive, but Percy was a good mechanic, and soon even that was a thing of the past. Course, it was still best to drive with the windows down, the inside of the car didn't come as clean as the outside.

First he went over to Leland to play, and in a few other near places. But he found only the New Delta out there, a New Delta that he painfully didn't know. And so it was in all the places he went. People wanted to hear songs of protest, songs against the war, and songs of freedom like 'We Shall Overcome'...

Chapter 26

Parchman, Again

When things settled down to almost normal, Delta began to move around a bit, but he always returned to Belzoni. He avoided Clarksdale and Chicago at all cost. One time he even went as far as California and New York. To be sure, the days of riding the rails were things of the past. To hobo was to take your life in your hands, but even the thought of all the dangers wasn't enough to take away the desire 'To reach up and grab iron'.

There was a thrill that made you feel good all over when you could wait in the bushes for a slow-moving freight, and when the time was right, you grabbed a hold of it. You grabbed iron, oh it was something to swing aboard an old steam engine freight. The new diesels just didn't have it.

So he paid his way.

However the time came when he had to go back to Chicago and the Little Delta. He had to say goodbye, and pay his respects to a dear old friend. 'It's a mean old world to try and live in all by yourself.'

Later, when the sad goodbyes were said, some of the old Bluesmen got together, and after playing 'Mean Oold World', they just mellowed down easy and played some of the songs that made him famous. They played all that night.

Oh, they did 'Juke, You're so Fine', 'Blues with a Feeling', 'Oh Baby', 'Blue Midnight' and all the many songs that folks loved to hear him do, as only he could do them. And just before dawn they did 'Blue Midnight', everyone playing their harps, and only one guitar holding the beat. Oh it was so beautiful.

Then again in August of 1976 he repeated that sad trip, so another great Legend of the Blues wouldn't have to go down that lonesome road all by himself.

Once again some of the old Bluesmen came together to play tribute to one of their own. One who had moved on up a little higher and was playing the Blues for the good Lord.

Oh baby, you don't have to go.

They started playing at a private home, and soon that home got too small, so they moved on down to the Little Queen of Clubs.

Now that was a most exciting time, they sang their sorrow and you could hear it all, even from the strings of the guitars, and the moaning of the harps. Some of the legendary Bluesmen were a little under the weather themselves, but they came and they stood side by side.

Once again the air was filled with the strange mellow melodies that were born in the heart of the Mississippi delta. From those legends of their times, came the enchanting melodies of 'Jimmie's Boogie', 'Ain't that Loving You Baby', 'Honest I Do', 'Hush-Hush', 'Big Boss Man', and they went on and on.

Before going back to the real delta, Delta Sonny just had to go back to Maxwell Street and see if what the others said was true. It was.

Maxwell Street had changed a lot. There were modern innovations all over the place that robbed that hallmark of market places of its basic character. And that was oh so sad. The faces of the hustlers, and con persons were undeniable. The quality of the products had slipped way down, and to add to all that, sadness.

The fine art and finesse of bargaining, or bartering for a pair of socks, or a 'gold' watch were joys of the past. My, how sad that was.

You know, after being with so many of his old buddies and their asking him to come back to the Little Delta and try again, he realised that his heart never left Chicago, the Little Delta, and the wonderful people who were driven from their second homeland, to settle with him on the South Side of Chicago. Goodness knows there were more people from his generation and environment of the Mississippi delta living in Chicago than there were living in the real delta.

So he promised them that he would go back down home, and set things to right, and when that was done he would come on back home to Chicago, the Little Delta, and the Little Queen of Clubs. Crazy Willie and LD were there, and they were very happy with Delta's decision to come back home so they could get together again, and on with their lives.

Willie Mae was married to her high-class doctor and she was Mrs Whatcha may call him, the Third. Delta went to the school and saw Jasmine during the break, and he was so happy, 'cause she called him 'Daddy'.

Jasmine told him that he was, and would always be 'her daddy'. Just talking with her lifted him up so high, his feet weren't touching the ground when he left her.

She hugged him, and promised that someday she would come to live with him, when she was old enough: 'Daddy, I love you.'

You know, sometime even when someone loves you, there is a lot of pain that goes along with that love. So it was with old Delta. The wound was wide open again. And he cried so much that he couldn't see where he was going. And that's the truth.

There was a new awareness to the real country Blues, and the men who had devoted their lives to that form of music. There were some of the great names on the white music scene that were grudgingly admitting that they used something from the music of the country Bluesmen to climb their ladder of success. That the foundation, and in a lot of cases the entire structure of their latest hit, had come from the Blues.

Even the guitar picker, who couldn't pick the guitar, secretly admitted that his roots was firmly seated in the country Blues, the material that he stole, or outright took.

Old Delta came to the correct conclusion that it was time for him to get on with the rest of his life.

179

Hurry down sunshine see what tomorrow brings
It may bring sunshine, or it may bring rain.
Lord, Lord, Lord!

Once he was back home in the delta, he discussed his returning to Chicago with his Mother and Percy. They both agreed wholeheartedly that it was time for Delta Sonny the Bluesman to sing again. So after setting everything right, and the last day before he was to leave, that morning Jessie got up early as was her usual thing, and she fixed one of his favourite meals for breakfast: fist biscuits, hard-fried home-cured ham, Brer rabbit molasses, and cold butter milk. Jessie and Percy had Louisiana-style coffee, instead of milk.

Well, even while eating that grand old delta breakfast, the thought of fresh neckbones and spaghetti flung a craving on Delta, and he asked her if she could fix him a pot of that delightful goodness, before he left for Chicago.

As it was, Jessie didn't have the fixings on hand, so it was necessary that they go into town to the supermarket

For some unknown reason, she tried to talk him out of the neckbones, saying that there were 'other things that she could fix, which he liked just as well'. And her mind and heart went to the graveyard where Mama Zula was sleeping, but for some other strange reason, the message wasn't clear. Just that she had a bad feeling about something. Matter of fact, Delta later admitted that he also had a bad feeling about going into town.

But he told himself that he couldn't go through the rest of his life being afraid of his own shadow. Even after, just before getting into town and along the lone stretch of highway, he clearly saw Mama Zula standing on the side of the road, and she had her head down, like she was in great sorrow.

He slowed down, and started to turn around. But the fool in him repeated that tired old bit about him going through the rest of his life afraid of shadows.

And before the cock would crow three times, hence, he had denied her three times.

Against his better judgement, Delta drove on into Belzoni. Now there was one particular store that Jessie liked to do her shopping,

180

and once they found a parking place on the parking lot they got out and went towards the store.

Well, as it was, there was a small group of college students in town for the purpose of registering black people to vote. And they had a table set up close to the entrance of the store in which Jessie liked to shop.

The group consisted of four young students, three pretty girls, one white, one Oriental, and one black. The fourth student was an intelligent-looking black youth.

There were also two adults, that looked to be teachers, or professors, and they were clearly in charge. One black male and one white male.

They were in Belzoni all the way from Philadelphia, Pennsylvania.

Well, what happened that day went something like this. There was also another group standing around the front of the store. Now, that second group was made up of some of the local white townsfolk. The size of the second group said clearly that they were not a representation of the townfolk, or the feelings of the town's people.

Because that second group of whites were heckling and taunting the group of students with a continuous stream of foul-mouthed words. And threatening to run the students out of town on a rail, to tar and feather them.

The rowdy group of whites were guzzling beer to bolster their lack of courage and human understanding.

When Delta, Jessie, and Percy approached the situation, two of the girls rushed up to them and inquired if they were registered to vote.

They were not registered, and Jessie said so. The girls promptly steered them over to the table, and immediately began to fill out the forms.

When Jessie took the pen to sign her name, two of the bigots from the heckling group ran over to the table, snatched the pen from Jessie and one of the men struck her and knocked her down. In spite of herself, Jessie screamed, more in anger than in pain.

That's when Delta spun around the man who struck his mother, and punched him in the nose. Percy grabbed the second red neck and held him till Delta could get around to doing him a job also.

What would you have done if Jessie were your mother?

Of, course that led to a free for all, with a lot of name-calling thrown in. The four college girls did themselves proud. When the other bigots attacked, they singled the young girls out; in their cowardice they thought the women would be easy pickings.

Oh how wrong they were, those young women flew into the loud-mouthed racists and made them back off, plus not to mention how foolish and inept they made the bunch of hecklers look to the town's people, who had watched the thing from the beginning.

Within minutes, the local fuzz was on the scene, almost like they were just waiting around the corner. The sheriff and his four deputies promptly arrested all the voter registration team and Delta.

Strangely enough, they didn't arrest Percy or Jessie, but told them to go on back home and not to say anything.

Even stranger was the fact that only Delta was charged with inciting a riot, striking a white minor. (The two men he punched out were both twenty years old, and not yet considered by law to be adults.)

Once they arrived at the local jail, the senior law official did listen to the one teacher who spoke for all his team, as he explained in detail what occurred.

And added to that, some of the town's people came in and agreed with the voter registration team. All charges were dropped, and both groups were told to 'Clear out, if later they were seen, then they would be arrested for sure'.

Jessie couldn't believe what she was hearing: they were free to go. My, wouldn't wonders ever cease. She couldn't understand what was happening, but she did know that it was to their best interest to get the hell out of there, asap.

She thanked the official, grabbed Delta and Percy as she headed for the door. Delta wasn't letting any grass grow under his feet either. They were lucky, and he decided that he would leave right away for Chicago. No sense in pushing his good fortune.

But you know, sometimes good fortune isn't all it's cracked up to be...

Just before Jessie, Delta, and Percy reached the door, another one of the local sheriff's deputies rushed through the door, and blocked their exit. He was closely followed by four Mississippi state troopers.

'That's him! That's Roosevelt Washington, or Delta Sonny.' The deputy pointed a finger at Delta. The last two state troopers in the door stopped and effectively barred the door so no one could leave.

The deputy who was pointing at Delta surely did know him, they had known each other since childhood. One of the state troopers came directly to where Delta and his family stood as if rooted to the spot.

Poor Jessie knew something was terribly wrong, something that they weren't going to just walk away from, no sir. Delta's stomach knotted up, and he was almost physically sick.

Old Trouble found him, and was fixing to walk all over him.

'Roosevelt Lincoln Washington, I'm arresting you for shooting two law officers over in Choctaw County.' One of the other state troopers slapped the cuffs on poor old Delta.

'Now, boy, don't you insult me by saying you didn't do it. We have six witnesses and four of them are coloured folks, so you can't scream that we're prejudiced. You shot them men sure as I'm standing here. Oh, it took us some time to run you down, but that's where good police work paid off.

'They got your Illinois licence tag number from that Buick outside that you thought you got away in. There's a bullet hole still in the trunk from one of the men you shot, just before he shot at you.

'We got your .38, with your prints all over it, as verified by the FBI and your old school, you know, Parchman. So you just come on and go on down to Jackson with us. There's a nice big cell waiting for you.

'Now, boy, don't you give me no trouble, 'cause I'm tired of you folk going up north and coming back here and causing all the trouble amongst the other good coloureds.

'I'm taking you in, one way or the other, now it's up to you.'

The big trooper said his piece, stepped back, and indicated to the other troopers holding Delta to take him out to their waiting cars.

Jessie started crying softly, and just rubbing her son's face. 'Sir, my son's been real sick and he came to me all out of his head. Sir, during the time that shooting happened RW was not himself, he was sick. He came to me just like a little baby child, and it was over three months before he even said a word.

'If he shot anybody he surely was out his head and didn't know what he was doing. Please, sir, believe me, he wouldn't shoot no law men.'

Jessie was pitifully begging.

'Please Mama, don't! I really don't know nothing about shooting anybody. Mama, I'm sorry to cause you nothing but trouble. Stand back and let these men do their jobs. Please.'

The teachers and students tried to come to his aid, but were stopped by the state troopers, who threatened them with interfering with officers in the discharge of their official duties. The local deputies were instructed to clear the office of everyone who had no need to be there.

Delta was loaded into one of the state trooper patrol cars, while one trooper brought the local sheriff up to date on what was going down. After that, the state troopers, with Delta in tow, drove away.

Percy helped Jessie into the car. Delta had already given him the keys and all the things he had on him. When Percy drove away from the kerb, both he and Jessie clearly saw Mama Zula standing in front of the police station. She seemed to be crying.

The trial in Jackson took only an hour. Oh, poor old Delta was sentenced to twenty years. Twenty years at hard labour, to be carried out at the Mississippi State Penitentiary, at PARCHMAN.

Mother don't you worry about your son.

However, because no one was killed, and the FBI and NAACP did some talking before the trial, the judge allowed that Delta would be 'eligible for parole after serving half his sentence, and with good behaviour'.

That would mean that he might be able to change his clothes sometime around 1985.

It was a Friday afternoon when Delta arrived back to hell, back to old Parchman Farm.

He looked up at Old Hannah, the sun, and his heart filled with the words:

> Go down ol Hannah don't you raise no mo
> If you raise in the morning you bring
> Judgement Day,
> Go down old Hannah.

One of the old guards came up to him and told him that he would be going back into the same tank he was in before. And if he was a 'good boy' he might make him a picket boss before too long.

> Black Betty's in the bottom, let your hammer ring.

Finally, old Delta couldn't hold back no longer, he just had to holler. Then he broke out and began to sing:

> The last thing I heard that po boy say was gimmie a cool drink
>   a water fo I die.
> Lord, Lord, gimmie a cool drink a water fo I die.

Epilogue

Let Your Hammer Ring

So it was that the great Bluesmen from all over the country came to Chicago. They came together because the word had gone out over the grapevine, and through the media there was going to be a 'jook to end all jooks'.

And all the great legends of the Blues were asked to come and sing a song. The jook would be held in the Little Delta, on the South Side, and at Soldier Field.

There, at that time, they would be able to pay homage to the birthplace of the country Blues, and the great men who carried the torch so high.

There would be stands, and open-air cooking just like there used to be on the old Maxwell Street, and down on the cotton plantations in Mississippi.

Most all of the old-fashioned delta cooking and foods would be available. The wonderful aroma of bar-b-cue spare ribs, and chittlings cooking will fill the air.

Crackling bread, pig's feet, red beans and rice, fried chicken and fist biscuits would be there to eat, all you had to do was ask for whatever you wanted.

And not to forget, Mississippi sweetbreads, chocolate cakes, and tater pies. There would be enough for all.

The country preacher would start the jook with a prayer, and everyone would stand and sing 'Precious Lord take my hand'.

Muddy Waters and Lightnin' Hopkins would be Masters of Ceremonies. All those who love the country Blues were asked to attend. There would be no price of admission at the gates but rather sealed containers, where each person would be asked to donate whatever he could afford to the eventual construction of a country Blues hall of fame.

And that hall would be raised to stand on the South Side in the Little Delta.

And it came to pass that the grandest jook of all was held not in Mississippi, which is the true birthplace of the country Blues, but rather in Chicago, which may be considered the midwife in attendance.

That is why the jook was held at Soldier Field on the South Side, and in the Little Delta.

Oh, I tell you! When that history-making day finally came, there wasn't a vacant seat in the entire stadium. The bandstand was specially designed and constructed like no other before it. It was round and covered with a halo of lights and television cameras.

It was also situated in the centre of the field, and designed to slowly rotate so that all those who came to witness that grand event could clearly see the Blues persons as they did their thing. The base of the stand was stationary, and with a special covered walkway so the performers could enter and exit the stage without being seen.

Oh, in addition to those inventive new ideas, there were also giant movie screens positioned so the audiences could see their favourite Blues person on screen as well as in person. And the sound system was state of the art.

A special place was set for the mayor, the families of those old Bluesmen who had already crossed over that great River, and for the one man who had certainly done more than any other man in history to bring the proud tradition of the country Blues to the people of our great nation, and to the world for that matter.

He would give the introduction to the occasion, and stand in as Master of Ceremonies when Muddy and Lightnin' were on stage singing.

Mr Robert Jackson was introduced and it was he who told everyone about how the Blues began, and where it all began, then he introduced the first medley of songs which were the original recordings of some of the granddaddies of them all. The voice of Blind Willie Johnson, followed by the voice of the Legend himself, Blind Lemon Jefferson. Then came Robert Johnson, Blind Willie McTell, Charlie Patton, Bessie Smith, Lillian Glinn and Leadbelly.

A hush fell over the crowd, and the feeling of honour and respect filled the air. It was just like Bessie Smith and Leadbelly were right there on that stage.

And the true believers could feel their majestic presence.

When the last sounds of Little Walter's 'Juke' faded away, it was replaced by the live voices of Brownie McGhee and Sonny Terry. They were already sitting in centre stage, their guitar and harp playing the melodies to 'Better Day'.

Muddy Waters introduced them to the very few for whom the introduction was necessary. Next they did 'Make a Little Money', and ended with their very own great version of that timeless old favourite, 'John Henry', that steel-driving man.

Now I don't rightly remember the order in which the great Bluesmen took the stage 'cause there were so many of them to sing. I just remember when old Howlin' Wolf got up there, the crowd was well into what was happening. He started with 'Red Rooster', then he did 'Going Down Slow', and finally 'Highway 49'.

Oh, the joint was rocking, and all the vendors were selling bar-b-cued ribs, and fish sandwiches, instead of hot dogs. And fresh-roasted goobers instead of peanuts, and slices of delta cracklin' bread, sweet bread, cake and tater pie, instead of cracker jacks.

Man and boy, the wonderful aroma of all that good delta cooking was enough to raise the dead, and had folk drooling all over themselves.

So while the good folk greased on down, the true legends of the Blues did the one thing they knew how to do best, and that was play the Blues.

The list of great names who came to contribute their part was endless. I saw some of them, to name only a few. There was:

John Lee Hooker, Sonny Boy Williamson, Pete Haycock, Phil Upchurch, Otis Rush, and the list went on and on.

Somewhere along the way, some of the old-timers got caught up in the music and they got up and showed the youngsters how to buck dance and do the slow drag.

BB King did 'How Long', 'I'm Going to Move to the Outskirts of Town', and of course he had to do 'The Thrill Is Gone'.

Joe Turner and Pete Johnson did 'Cherry Red', 'Piney Brown', and 'Wee Wee Baby'. John Lee Hooker did 'Bottle Up and Go', 'It Serves You Right to Suffer', 'Decoration Day', and 'Country Boy'.

When it was Lightnin's turn he did 'Awful Dream', 'Worried Life Blues', and 'Baby Please Don't Go'.

Now Muddy came on with 'My Home Is in the Delta', 'Born Lover', 'Mojo Hand', 'Rock Me', and he did some for the legend who was not able to do them himself at that time, like: 'You Don't Have to Go', 'Honest I Do', 'Big Boss Man' and 'Hush Hush'.

The music was sweet, sometimes sad, and all the time mellow. There were some African Americans who were pleasantly surprised, so very happy and mostly downright overjoyed to see, hear, and feel the Blues as the Blues was presented at that jook.

And I am sad to say there were too many black, African Americans, who didn't have the slightest idea that what was happening was a most important part of their own beautiful heritage/inheritance.

And yes, there was a lot of pride, new found and old (I have it already). That kind of pride which is very much like that old-time religion.

Matter of fact, there were many of those who attended who, when asked, said there were times when they felt like they were at an old-fashioned Revival.

The Blues were so good, the Bluesmen so great, that the moment really thrilled the soul. Most of the time it was hard to sit down, they wanted to get up and dance, to swing and sway with that great music that was as much a part of them, of their very makeup, as the colour of their skin, or the texture of their hair.

In that way, they were probably as close to their ancient and enchanting heritage as they would ever be. Yes, by the grace of the African gods, they were attending a sweet revival, a revival to re-ignite the flame of African pride in their minds, hearts and souls.

And so, thousands of wonderful people who came to hear the

Blues, heard the Blues and were refreshed. They would leave with a better understanding of 'Why I sing the Blues'.

And for those thousands of non-Africans, some of them who came from as far away as Paris, France, Holland, Japan, Germany, and Canada, it was a time for them to be refreshed and understand even better that which was being presented.

To understand the true greatness of that pure American art form.

The crowd was treated to such old greats as 'Stack-o-Lee', 'CC Rider', 'Haunting', 'Black Snake Moan' and 'Good Evening Little Schoolgirl'.

Just about the end of the jook, there were times that three or four, maybe even more of the Bluesmen would do a number together. Now that's when they did some of the old prison work songs, or hollers, from the chain gangs, cotton pickers, and wheelers on the levee. Like 'Go Down Old Hanaha', the 'Levee-Camp Holler', and many, many more such work songs.

Even some of the good folk who had no idea of what it was like on a chain gang couldn't help but know that some of the old Bluesmen had once worn the striped suit and had the shackles with the ball and chain on their legs.

You know the dictionary explains that a prison is a 'place where criminals are confined'. But you gotta know that definition isn't always true.

Well, as it is with all bad things, and good things, there had to be an end. So when the last group filled the stage and played Little Walter's 'Blue Midnight' and the Blues stopped, the jook was over. The happy people went their respective ways.

Soldier Field was again empty of the crowd, except for the maintenance crews, clean-up crews and technicians. That's when they said the miracle continued.

All the Soldier Field personnel who were there at that time solemnly swore that after the sound system was de-activated everyone there clearly heard the distinct voice of Leadbelly singing and playing his guitar, as he sang: 'Good night, Irene'.